AF568100

ALEPH *olio*

---

LOVE AND LUST

One of the meanings of the word 'olio' is 'a miscellany'. The books in the Aleph Olio series contain a selection of the finest writing to be had on a variety of Indian themes—the great cities, aspects of culture and civilization, and other uniquely Indian phenomena. Filled with insights and haunting evocations of a country of unrivalled complexity, beauty, tragedy and mystery, each Aleph Olio book presents India in ways that it has seldom been seen before.

Also in Aleph Olio

*The Essence of Delhi*

*In a Violent Land*

*Notes from the Hinterland*

Forthcoming in Aleph Olio

*Ways of Dying*

*The Book of Kings*

# LOVE AND LUST

*Stories and Essays*

ALEPH BOOK COMPANY
An independent publishing firm
promoted by ***Rupa Publications India***

First published in India in 2019
by Aleph Book Company
7/16 Ansari Road, Daryaganj
New Delhi 110 002



ISBN: 978-93-88292-52-8

1 3 5 7 9 10 8 6 4 2



Printed at Replika Press Pvt. Ltd, India

*Desire can be a delicate thing*
*or so the punishments*
*suggest.*
*Who needs as much as the naked*
*breast? Lust*
*is aroused by a wrist*
*revealed,*
*the hollow at the neck,*
*the ankle-bone*
*half-concealed.*

*The guardians of our need*
*patrol the streets, fired*
*with pure passion,*
*eager to find the flesh*
*unsealed, frantic*
*to mete out justice,*

*Oh delicious,*
*exquisite pleasure, to punish*
*the object of our desire.*

—From 'Object' by IMTIAZ DHARKER

# A NOTE ON STYLE

As the various stories and essays in this book have been excerpted from books that have their own styles of spelling Indian words and proper nouns, no attempt has been made to standardize the text according to the Aleph house style. The only stylistic rules that have been observed throughout the book are that British spellings have been used and Indian words have not been italicized.

## CONTENTS

one

~

## A SUITABLE BOY*

## VIKRAM SETH

Mrs Rupa Mehra came breathlessly through the door. She had been crying in the tonga. The tonga-wallah, concerned that such a decently dressed lady should be weeping so openly, had tried to keep up a monologue in order to pretend that he hadn't noticed, but she had now gone through not only her embroidered handkerchief but her reserve handkerchief as well.

'Oh my daughter!' she said, 'oh, my daughter.'

Savita said, 'Yes, Ma?' She was shocked to see her mother's tear-streaked face.

'Not you,' said Mrs Rupa Mehra. 'Where is that shameless Lata?'

Savita sensed that their mother had discovered something. But what? And how much? She moved instinctively towards her to calm her down.

'Ma, sit down, calm down, have some tea,' said Savita,

*Extracted from *A Suitable Boy*

guiding Mrs Rupa Mehra, who seemed quite distracted, to her favourite armchair.

'Tea! Tea! More and more tea!' said Mrs Rupa Mehra in resistant misery.

Savita went and told Mateen to get some tea for the two of them.

'Where is she? What will become of us all? Who will marry her now?'

'Ma, don't over-dramatize things,' said Savita soothingly. 'It will blow over.'

Mrs Rupa Mehra sat up abruptly. 'So you knew! You knew! And you didn't tell me. And I had to learn this from strangers.' This new betrayal engendered a new bout of sobbing. Savita squeezed her mother's shoulders, and offered her another handkerchief. After a few minutes of this, Savita said:

'Don't cry, Ma, don't cry. What did you hear?'

'Oh, my poor Lata—is he from a good family? I had a sense something was going on. Oh God! What would her father have said if he had been alive? Oh, my daughter.'

'Ma, his father teaches mathematics at the university. He's a decent boy. And Lata's a sensible girl.'

Mateen brought the tea in, registered the scene with deferential interest, and went back towards the kitchen.

Lata walked in a few seconds later. She had taken a book to the banyan grove, where she had sat down undisturbed for a while, lost in Wodehouse and her own enchanted thoughts. Two more days, one more day, and she would see Kabir again.

She was unprepared for the scene before her, and stopped in the doorway.

'Where have you been, young lady?' demanded Mrs Rupa Mehra, her voice quivering with anger.

'For a walk,' faltered Lata.

'Walk? Walk?' Mrs Rupa Mehra's voice rose to a crescendo. 'I'll give you walk.'

Lata's mouth flew open, and she looked at Savita. Savita shook both her head and her right hand slightly, as if to say that it was not she who had given her away.

'Who is he?' demanded Mrs Rupa Mehra. 'Come here. Come here at once.'

Lata looked at Savita. Savita nodded.

'Just a friend,' said Lata, approaching her mother.

'Just a friend! A friend! And friends are for holding hands with? Is this what I brought you up for? All of you—and is this—'

'Ma, sit down,' said Savita, for Mrs Rupa Mehra had half risen out of her chair.

'Who told you?' asked Lata. 'Hema's Taiji?'

'Hema's Taiji? Hema's Taiji? Is she in this too?' exclaimed Mrs Rupa Mehra with new indignation. 'She lets those girls run around all over the place with flowers in their hair in the evening. Who told me? The wretched girl asks me who told me. No one told me. It's the talk of the town, everyone knows about it. Everyone thought you were a good girl with a good reputation—and now it is too late. Too late,' she sobbed.

'Ma, you always say Malati is such a nice girl,' said Lata by way of self-defence. 'And she has friends like that—you know that—everyone knows that.'

'Be quiet! Don't answer me back! I'll give you two tight slaps. Roaming around shamelessly near the dhobi-ghat and having a gala time.'

'But Malati—'

'Malati! Malati! I'm talking about you, not about Malati. Studying medicine and cutting up frogs—' Mrs Rupa Mehra's voice rose once more. 'Do you want to be like her? And lying to your mother. I'll never let you go for a walk again. You'll stay in this house, do you hear? Do you hear?' Mrs Rupa Mehra had stood up.

'Yes, Ma,' said Lata, remembering with a twinge of shame that she had had to lie to her mother in order to meet Kabir. The enchantment was being torn apart; she felt alarmed and miserable.

'What's his name?'

'Kabir,' said Lata, growing pale.

'Kabir what?'

Lata stood still and didn't answer. A tear rolled down her cheek.

Mrs Rupa Mehra was in no mood for sympathy. What were all these ridiculous tears? She caught hold of Lata's ear and twisted it. Lata gasped.

'He has a name, doesn't he? What is he—Kabir Lal, Kabir Mehra—or what? Are you waiting for the tea to get cold? Or have you forgotten?'

Lata closed her eyes.

'Kabir Durrani,' she said, and waited for the house to come tumbling down.

The three deadly syllables had their effect. Mrs Rupa Mehra clutched at her heart, opened her mouth in silent horror, looked unseeingly around the room, and sat down.

Savita rushed to her immediately. Her own heart was beating far too fast.

One last faint possibility struck Mrs Rupa Mehra. 'Is he a Parsi?' she asked weakly, almost pleadingly. The thought was odious but not so calamitously horrifying. But a look at Savita's face told her the truth.

'A Muslim!' said Mrs Rupa Mehra more to herself now than to anyone else. 'What did I do in my past life that I have brought this upon my beloved daughter?'

Savita was standing near her and held her hand. Mrs Rupa Mehra's hand was inert as she stared in front of her. Suddenly she became aware of the gentle curve of Savita's stomach, and fresh horrors came to her mind.

She stood up again. 'Never, never, never—' she said.

By now Lata, having conjured up the image of Kabir in her mind, had gained a little strength. She opened her eyes. Her tears had stopped and there was a defiant set to her mouth.

'Never, never, absolutely not—dirty, violent, cruel, lecherous—'

'Like Talat Khala?' demanded Lata. 'Like Uncle Shafi? Like the Nawab Sahib of Baitar? Like Firoz and Imtiaz?'

'Do you want to marry him?' cried Mrs Rupa Mehra in a fury.

'Yes!' said Lata, carried away, and angrier by the second.

'He'll marry you—and next year he'll say "Talaq talaq talaq" and you'll be out on the streets. You obstinate, stupid girl! You should drown yourself in a handful of water for sheer shame.'

'I *will* marry him,' said Lata, unilaterally.

'I'll lock you up. Like when you said you wanted to become a nun.'

Savita tried to intercede.

'You go to your room!' said Mrs Rupa Mehra. 'This isn't good for you.' She pointed her finger, and Savita, not used to being ordered about in her own home, meekly complied.

'I wish I had become a nun,' said Lata. 'I remember Daddy used to tell us we should follow our own hearts.'

'Still answering back?' said Mrs Rupa Mehra, infuriated by the mention of Daddy. 'I'll give you two tight slaps.'

She slapped her daughter hard, twice, and instantly burst into tears.

two

~

# TANG

## SAADAT HASAN MANTO

*Translated from the Urdu by Nasreen Rehman*

They were the same old monsoon days. Beyond the window the rain was pouring down on the peepul leaves in the same old way. On the spring mattress of a teak bed, now pushed away from the window a little to this side, a Ghatan was clinging to Randhir. Beyond the window in night's radiant darkness the bathed peepul leaves were shimmering like jhumkas and that Ghatan was clinging to Randhir like a persistent shiver down his spine.

It was early evening. After reading all the news and advertisements in an English newspaper he had stepped out on to the balcony leisurely when he spotted the Ghatan standing under the tamarind tree to escape the rain. It seemed she worked in the rope factory next door. He coughed and cleared his throat to attract her attention and finally with a wave of his hand he called her upstairs.

For several days he had been feeling very lonesome. There was a time when almost all the Christian girls in Bombay were available to him at affordable rates. Now, due to the war some had joined the Women's Auxiliary Force, while others had opened dance schools in the Fort area where entry was restricted to gora soldiers. Randhir was miserable and the primary reason for his misery was that Christian girls had turned into gold dust. To crown it all, although Randhir was far more cultivated, educated, fit and handsome in comparison with gora men, the doors of most pleasure houses in Fort were closed to him because of the colour of his skin. Before the war, Randhir had physical relations with Christian girls quite regularly in the areas around Nagpara and Taj Hotel. He knew for sure that he was far better informed about the niceties of such matters than the Christian lads with whom these girls had brief flings before they married some imbecile or the other.

Randhir had called the Ghatan upstairs with a wave of his hand to seek quiet revenge on Hazel for her new-found hoity-toityness. Hazel lived in the flat below. She set out every morning, wearing her uniform with a khaki cap set at a cocky angle on her short hair, strutting along the pavement expecting all passers-by to fall at her feet like doormats for her to walk over.

Several times Randhir had tried to understand his reasons for his attraction to all these Christian girls. Undoubtedly, they had no qualms about displaying their bodies to their advantage, or discussing the chaos surrounding their lives—even talking about their old beaus. And on hearing a dance tune they loved to shake a leg. All this was very well, but any woman could have had these qualities.

When Randhir had summoned the Ghatan upstairs, he was not in the least bit sure that he'd ask her to sleep with him. But when he saw her drenched clothes he thought 'What if the poor girl catches pneumonia', so he said to her, 'Take these clothes off, you'll catch a chill.' She understood what he meant, because shame was reflected in her eyes; but when Randhir handed her his white dhoti, she gave the matter some thought and untied her kashta, which looked filthier after getting drenched in the rain. She untied it carefully keeping a part of her body covered as she wrapped the white dhoti around her hips. She proceeded to take off her tight-fitting choli by undoing the knot she had tied by pulling its two front corners together. It had sunk into the grimy cleavage of her small but firm breasts. She kept trying to undo the knot with the help of her chipped nails, but it too had become tighter. Fed up and accepting defeat she turned to Randhir and said something in Marathi which meant, 'What should I do? I can't undo it.'

Randhir sat down next to her and tried to undo the knot. Exasperated, he took one end of her choli in one hand and the other end in the other and pulled hard. Suddenly, the knot gave way. Randhir's hands fell back revealing two pulsating breasts. For a moment Randhir felt like a nimble potter whose hands had kneaded and shaped the soft clay of this girl's breasts into two exquisite bowls. Her young breasts had the same compelling ripe moisture and cool warmth of fresh unfired clay as it leaves the hands of a potter. These young, unblemished breasts exuded a peculiar lustre like dark wheat lit from below by a faint flicker of light creating an extraordinary elusive glow. The undulation of her breasts on her body looked like lamps aflame in the muddy waters of a pond.

Yes, they were the same old monsoon days and beyond the window the peepul leaves were shimmering. Two items of clothing belonging to the Ghatan, soaked in rain, were lying in a filthy pile on the floor and she was clinging to Randhir. The heat of her grimy naked body stirred in Randhir's body a sensation akin to one he had experienced in deep midwinter when bathing in the filthy piping hot hammam run by nais—the local barbers.

All night long she clung to Randhir. It was as though their

bodies had merged into each other; they barely exchanged a few words because their breath, their lips and hands communicated whatever they wanted to say or hear. As Randhir's hands moved across her breasts like a gentle breeze, her small nipples and areolae awakened to his touch creating such tremors of ecstasy in the Ghatan's body that for a moment Randhir found himself shivering.

Randhir was familiar with these sensations and had spent many such nights with his chest close to the hard or soft breasts of several girls. He had slept with tenacious girls who wrapped themselves around him as they shared intimate secrets about their personal lives that should have remained hidden. He had physical relations with girls who did all the hard work and gave him no trouble—but this Ghatan he had summoned with the wave of a hand, as she stood getting drenched under a tamarind tree, was very different.

All night Randhir could smell an unfamiliar odour from her. An odour that was both agreeable and foul. All night long it permeated his senses—from her underarms, her breasts, her hair, her stomach, from every part of her body, this odour that was both agreeable and foul was present in every breath that he took. All night long he kept thinking that although this Ghatan was so close to him, under no circumstances would he have felt so close to her had this odour not drifted from her naked body and crept into every nook and cranny of his heart and mind, penetrating his old and new thoughts.

The odour had fused Randhir and the girl into one for a night. They descended into the innermost recesses of each other's beings, where they melded into a sensation of pure human ecstasy—a sensation that although transient was eternal—that in mid-flight stood still like a bird flying high, so high into the blue sky that it seemed immobile.

Randhir understood the odour ensuing from every pore of the Ghatan's body, but he could not describe it. It was a bit like the smell of earth with water sprinkled on it...but no—that was different. There was nothing synthetic about it—it was real like the intimacy shared between a man and a woman—real and eternal.

Randhir couldn't stand the smell of sweat. Usually, after his bath he dusted his underarms etc., with powder or used a preparation to repress the smell of sweat. It's astonishing that several times, yes, several times when he kissed the Ghatan's hairy armpits he was not repelled but experienced a curious pleasure. The soft hair in her armpits moist with sweat, was exuding the same tang. Randhir felt he knew the tang, recognized it and understood what it meant, but could not describe it to anybody.

They were the same old monsoon days when he had looked out beyond the same window at peepul leaves shimmering in the rain. The air was full of the same rustle and bustle of sounds. The darkness had a hint of light because starlight had descended to touch the raindrops. It was like the same old monsoon days when Randhir's room had just one teak bed but now there was another next to it—with a new dressing table in the corner.

They were the same old monsoon days and the weather was the same, because starlight had descended to touch the raindrops. But the air was full of a strong scent of the attar of henna. The other spring bed was empty. And on the bed on which Randhir lay face downwards looking out of the window at the dance of the raindrops on the shimmering peepul leaves, it seemed a milky white girl had fallen asleep failing in her attempt to conceal her naked body. Lying on the other bed was her red silk shalwar with a bauble dangling down from its crimson drawstring. Her gold floral shirt, bodice, knickers and dupatta—all red—very red—were steeped in the attar of henna.

Silver stardust clung to the girl's black hair. The rose of the rouge on her powdered cheeks combined with particles of stardust created an unusual hue—wan and lifeless. The raw colour of her bodice had bled on her white bosom leaving red marks here and there. Her breasts were as white as milk with a hint of blue in it. Her underarms were shaved, giving them a grey cloudy impression. Randhir looked at this girl several times and each time he felt he had taken her out like books and china crockery from an old wooden trunk after pulling out the nails that were fastening it—because just as over time books and china acquire marks and scratches due to movement or pressure, this girl had several marks and scratches all over her body.

Untying the strings of her tight-fitting bodice Randhir found marks under her soft breasts and around her waist where the tight drawstring of her shalwar had dug into her flesh. Her heavy pointed gem studded gold necklace had grazed her bosom in several places as though it had been scratched by long nails. They were the same old monsoon days and raindrops falling on the smooth and gentle peepul leaves were creating the same sound that Randhir had heard all through that night. It was the same lovely season with a gentle cool breeze but mixed with a strong attar of henna.

For a long time Randhir's hands moved across the white breasts of this milky white girl. He felt several responses including shivers running through several parts of her milky white body. When he pressed his chest close to hers Randhir was aware of every pore of the girl's body responding to his touch; but where was that cry that Randhir had smelt in the tang of that Ghatan's body. A cry far more compelling than that of a baby thirsting for milk—a cry that had crossed the sound barrier and become soundless.

Randhir was looking out through the window with iron bars. The peepul leaves were shimmering very near him, but he was looking far beyond them into the distance where mixed with clouds the colour of mud he was able to see a faint glow like the one he had seen in that Ghatan's bosom—a hidden glow like a secret that is revealed.

Lying by Randhir's side was a girl whose milky white body was yielding like dough kneaded with milk and ghee. The body was asleep and exuding a tired smell of the attar of henna. Randhir disliked this fading aroma drawing its last breath. There was something strangely sour about it, like burps caused by indigestion—miserable, pasty and drained.

Randhir looked at the girl who lay by his side. Her body seemed like white flecks that rise and stand still on rancid milk—the girl's sensuality was stagnant. The odour that the Ghatan's body exuded so naturally and effortlessly was embedded in Randhir's mind. That odour was far lighter yet more pervasive than the attar of henna. Without any desire to be smelt, it permeated the senses involuntarily and reached its real destination.

Randhir made made one last attempt and stroked the girl's milky white body, but he did not feel a shudder. His brand-new wife, the daughter of a first-class magistrate, was educated and had a BA degree. In her college days she was the heartthrob of countless boys, but she was unable to make Randhir's pulse race. In the fading smell of henna he was seeking the same old monsoon days with peepul leaves shimmering in the rain beyond the window and the same odour emanating from the Ghatan's grimy body.

three

~

# A LITTLE KITTEN

## KAMALA DAS

When they had finally settled themselves down after weeks of honeymooning in a small flat at Dadar, she told her husband that she felt miserable and lonely from eight in the morning to six in the evening while he worked in his insurance firm at the heart of the city. If only you could get me a pet, she murmured, nestling closer to his chest, a little kitten, even a kitten would be such a comfort... And, he threw back his head and laughed. What a sweet and innocent creature he had married! He tickled her until she rolled over on their double bed and screamed out for mercy. You are killing me, please stop, PLEASE STOP. Then, he began to lick her toes, mumbling, you see, I am your kitten, I am your little kitten.

After three months of ardour, they began to quarrel. Nothing very serious, of course. Just a few probing queries regarding his relationship with Miss Nadkar, his secretary, and his mysterious silences that would last for hours.

Speak to me, I cannot bear these silences. Leave me alone, he would say and disappear into the bathroom.

One day, she climbed upon a stool and peeped into the bathroom through the ventilator. He was seated on the edge of the tub, frowning. What are you doing there, she shouted at him. He got up and pulled the ventilator shut. It nearly snapped off her fingers. No wonder she was angry and frustrated.

When they were on the best of terms she used to take a bath in the evening after tea and buy a jasmine strand from the flowerboy to hang from her long plait. She had naturally pink cheeks but on tiring days when she saw herself pale she cheated a little with a touch of rouge which she kept hidden away. When Miss Nadkar was unwittingly drawn into the orbit of their life together, she stopped taking the evening bath. The flowerboy went away disappointed.

Even the old Maharashtrian woman who used to wash the vessels for her in the morning began to wonder what had gone wrong. She had lost her bridal freshness. There was a new crease on her brow which sliced the red bindi in two halves. Pimples began to form on her cheeks. She found herself worrying about her digestion.

Then, one day he came home dead drunk after attending an office dinner. She tore her wedding saree into shreds. She grew frighteningly hysterical. Would you like to visit your parents for a month, he asked her. You look as if you need a change. She was alarmed. She went to look at her face secretly in the bathroom mirror. He was speaking the truth. She had lost the glow which she had before she settled down at Bombay. They were living close to a mill. She felt that the smoke from its chimney was darkening her skin. Yes, I need a change, she told him. But you will have to come with me...

He gave for the first time a birthday gift to his secretary because he had begun to compare her with his petulant little wife. Miss Nadkar was serene. In fact, he had once heard the clerks teasingly calling her Her Serene Highness. He thought it clever of the clerks. When he gave her an ivory figurine on her birthday, Miss Nadkar blushed very nicely and murmured: You shouldn't have spent so much money on me... He had done it on an impulse. After all, he was not the demonstrative kind. And she was Miss Nadkar to him although once she had asked him to call her by her name, Indira. I heard that you were planning to leave us soon Miss Nadkar, he said. The office will miss you. She blushed again. The marriage will take place only in December, she said. My fiancé will come from Canada in October. Still four months to go. And looking up into his eyes, she flashed a smile, a gleaming jet of a smile that made his stomach quiver.

That was their first evening together. They went to dark, smoke-filled restaurants and always took the corner table where they could sit half-concealed behind potted cacti. At home, his wife sulked and lost her looks thinking unkind thoughts incessantly. Once or twice, she put all her silks inside a trunk and decided to go back to Dharwar, but he dissuaded her. What will your parents say, he asked her.

One day, when he came back home, warily crossing the hall to go to their bedroom, he found his little wife seated before her dressing table brushing her wavy hair. She turned her face to smile at him. He was taken aback. She looked so pink and healthy. There was a gleam in her dark eyes, a secret message for the male. He rushed forward to embrace her. You look so pretty, he said. So pretty and happy. Then he saw above her breasts a long red scratch. What happened, he asked her. Did you find yourself a kitten? He looked around. Perhaps it was hiding somewhere in the kitchen. Is it a stray, he asked her. She kept silent. She was looking over his head to a spot in the dusky sky. What are you staring at, he asked her, I don't see anything there but some clouds, some smoke...

four

~

# LAAJWANTI

## RAJINDER SINGH BEDI

*Translated from the Urdu by Muhammad Umar Memon*

*Touch the leaves of the laajwanti,*
*they curl and wither away.*

After Partition, when countless wounded people had finally cleaned the gore from their bodies, they turned their attention to those who had not suffered bodily but had been wounded in their hearts.

Rehabilitation committees were formed in every neighbourhood and side street and the campaign to help the victims acquire business, land, and homes for themselves got underway with much enthusiasm. There was one programme, though, which seemed to have escaped notice. It concerned the rehabilitation of abducted women. Its rallying cry was 'Rehabilitate them in your hearts!' It was bitterly opposed by Narain Bawa's temple and the conservatives who lived in and around it.

A committee was formed in the Mulla Shakur neighbourhood near the temple to get the programme off the ground. Babu Sundar Lal was elected its secretary by a majority of eleven votes and the Vakil Sahib its president. It was the opinion of the old petition writer of the Chauki Kalan district—in which other well-regarded individuals of the neighbourhood concurred with him—that no one could be expected to work more passionately for the cause than Sundar Lal, because his own wife, Laaju—Laajwanti—too had been abducted.

Early in the morning when Babu Sundar Lal and his companions Rasaloo and Neki Ram used to make their rounds through the streets singing in unison, *Touch the leaves of the laajwanti, /they curl and wither away*! Sundar Lal's voice would fade. Walking along in silence he would think about Laajwanti—who knows where she might be? In what condition? What would she be thinking of him? Would she ever come back?—and his feet would falter on the cobblestone pavement.

But by now things had reached a point where he had stopped even thinking about Laajwanti. His pain was no longer just his; it had become part of the world's anguish. And to spare himself its devastation he had thrown himself headlong into serving the people. All the same, every time he joined his companions in that song, he couldn't help wondering at how delicate the human heart is. The slightest thing could hurt it. Exactly like the laajwanti plant, whose leaves curl up at the barest touch. Well, that may be. But for his own part, he had never spared any effort in treating his own Laajwanti as badly as possible. He would beat her on the flimsiest pretext, taking exception to the way she got up, the way she sat down, the way she cooked food—anything and everything.

Laaju was a slender and agile village girl. Too much sun had turned her skin quite dark, and a nervous energy informed her movements, which brought to mind the fluid grace of a dewdrop rolling like mercury on a leaf: now to one side, now to the other. Her slim build, which was more a sign of health than its absence, worried Sundar Lal at first, but when he observed how well she could take all manner of adversity, including even physical abuse, he progressively increased his mistreatment of her, quite forgetting that past a certain limit anyone's patience is sure to run out. Laajwanti, too, had contributed her share in obscuring the perception of such a limit. She wasn't, by nature, one to dwell on her anguish for too long. A simple smile from Sundar Lal following the worst fight, and she was unable to stop her giggles: 'If you beat me ever again, I'll never speak to you!'

It was obvious she had already forgotten all about the fights and beatings. That's how husbands treat their wives—she knew this truth as well as any other village girl. If a woman showed the slightest independence, the girls themselves would be the first to disapprove. 'Ha, what kind of man is he? Can't even keep his little woman in line!' The physical abuse men subjected their wives to had even made it into the women's songs. Laaju herself used to sing:

*Marry a city boy?—No sir, not me.*
*Look at his boots, and my waist is so narrow.*

Nonetheless, at the very first opportunity she had fallen in love with just such a city boy, Sundar Lal, who had first come to her village as part of a wedding party and had whispered into the groom's ear, 'Your sister-in-law is pretty hot stuff, yaar! Your wife must be quite a dish too!'

Laajwanti had overheard him. She took no notice at all of his large, heavy boots, and forgot all about her own narrow waist.

Such were the memories that Sundar Lal recalled during his early morning rounds with his companions. He would say to himself, 'If I could get another chance, just one more chance, I'd rehabilitate Laaju in my heart. I'd show the people that these poor women are hardly to blame for their abduction, their victimization by lecherous rioters. A society which is unable to accept and rehabilitate these innocent women is rotten to the core, fit only to be destroyed.'

Sundar Lal would plead with the people to take these women under their roof and give them the same status which any woman, any mother, daughter, sister, or wife enjoyed. He would urge the families never to mention, even to hint at the things the poor women had to suffer, because their hearts were already wounded, already fragile, like the leaves of the touch-me-not plant, ready to curl up at the merest touch.

The Mulla Shakur Rehabilitation of Hearts Committee took out many early morning processions to put its programme into effect. The wee hours of the morning were the most feasible time for their activity: no human noise, no traffic snarls. Even the dogs, after an exhausting night-long watch, would be asleep at this hour, as they lay curled up inside the tandoors long since gone cold. And people, huddled in their beds, would wake up to mumble drowsily, 'Oh, that group again!'

People listened to Sundar Lal Babu's propaganda, sometimes with patience, sometimes with irritation. Women who had made it safely to this side of the border lay loosely in their beds, while their husbands, lying stiff beside them, mumbled protests against the noise kicked up by the morning rally, or a child somewhere opened its eyes for a moment and fell back to sleep, taking the doleful petition of 'Rehabilitate them in your hearts' for a lullaby.

Words which enter the ear so early in the morning rarely fail to produce an effect. They reverberate in the mind the entire day, and even if their underlying meaning is not plain, one nonetheless finds oneself repeating them. So, thanks to this effect, when Miss Mridula Sara Bai secured the exchange of abducted women between India and Pakistan, some people in the Mulla Shakur neighbourhood willingly took their women back. They went to receive them outside the city at Chauki Kalan. For a while the abducted women and their relatives faced each other in awkward silence. Then, with their heads bent low, they returned to pick up the pieces of their lives and rebuild their homes. Meanwhile Rasaloo, Neki Ram and Sundar Lal rooted for them with cries, now of 'Long Live Mahendar Singh!' now of 'Long Live Sohan Lal!' They kept it up until their throats went dry.

But there were some abducted women whose husbands, parents, or siblings refused even to recognize them. As far as their families were concerned, they should have killed themselves. They should have taken poison to save their virtue. Or jumped into a well. Cowards—to cling to life so tenaciously!

Hundreds, indeed thousands, of women had in fact killed themselves to save their honour. But what could they know of the courage it took just to live on? What could they know of the icy stares it took for the survivors to look death in the face, in a world where even their husbands refused to recognize them? One or another of the abducted repeats her name to herself: 'Suhagwanti'—she who has suhag, the affection of her husband. She spots her brother in the crowd and says only this one final time, 'Even you, Bihari, refuse to recognize me! I took you in my lap and fed you when you were small.' Bihari wants to slip away, but he looks at his parents and freezes, who steel their hearts and look expectantly at Narain Bawa, who in turn looks in utter helplessness at the sky—which has no reality, which is merely an optical illusion, the limit beyond which our eyes do not reach.

Laaju, however, was not among the abducted women Miss Sara Bai brought back in the exchange. Sundar Lal, balanced precariously between hope and despair, saw the last girl come down from the military truck. Subsequently, with quiet determination, he redoubled his efforts in advancing the work of his Committee. No longer only in the mornings, the Committee took out an evening rally as well, and now and then also held meetings at which the old barrister, Kalka Parshad Sufi, the Committee's president, held forth in his raspy, asthmatic voice, with Rasaloo always tending his duties beside him, holding the spittoon. Strange sounds would pour out from the loudspeaker: 'kha-ba-ba-ba, kha-

kha…' Next, Neki Ram would get up to say something. But whatever he said or quoted from the Shastras or Puranas served only to contradict his point. Just then Sundar Lal would move in to salvage the situation. But he couldn't manage more than a couple of sentences. His voice would become progressively hoarser and tears would roll down his cheeks. He would give up and sit down. A strange silence would sweep over the audience. Sundar Lal Babu's two sentences, which sprang from the depths of his heart, affected them more than all the oratory eloquence of the old barrister Kalka Parshad Sufi. But the people shed a few tears then and there, which eased their hearts, and returned home, as empty-headed as ever.

One day the Committee-wallahs started out on their preaching mission early in the evening and ended up in an area long known to be a conservative stronghold. Seated on a cement platform around a peepul tree outside the temple, the faithful were listening to stories from the Ramayana. Narain Bawa was narrating the episode in which a washerman had thrown his wife out of the house saying, 'I'm no Raja Ramchandar, who would take Sita back after she had spent so many years with Ravan.' Which led Ramchandarji to order the virtuous Sita out of the house even though she was with child.

'Can you find a better example of Ram Raj?' asked Narain Bawa. 'True Ram Raj is one in which a washerman's words too receive the utmost consideration.'

The rally had by now reached the temple and it stopped to listen to the Ramayana story and pious hymns. Sundar Lal caught the last few words and retorted, 'We don't want Ram Raj, Bawa.'

Angry voices shot up from the throng of the faithful:

'Be quiet!'

'Who do you think you are?'

'Shut up!'

But Sundar Lal, undaunted, moved forward. 'Nobody can stop me from speaking!' he shouted back.

To which he received a fresh volley of equally angry words—'Quiet!' 'We won't let you speak!'—and from a corner, even the threat, 'We'll kill you!'

Narain Bawa said to him gently, 'Sundar Lal, my dear, you don't understand the rules and regulations of the Shastras.'

'But I do understand one thing, Bawa. And it is that even a washerman could be heard in Ram Raj, while its champions today won't even listen to Sundar Lal.'

The very people who a minute ago had gotten up determined to put him in his place quickly sat down, sweeping away the peepul fruits which had meanwhile fallen on their seats, and said, 'All right, let's hear him out.'

Both Rasaloo and Neki Ram spurred Sundar Lal on, who said, 'No doubt Shri Ram was our great leader. But why is it, Bawaji, that he believed the washerman but not his own wife, the greatest Maharani ever?'

Narain Bawa explained, putting a novel spin on it. 'Sita was his own wife. It would appear, Sundar Lal, that you have not realized the importance of this fact.'

'Yes, Bawa,' Sundar Lal Babu said, 'there are many things in this world that I don't understand. But as I look at it, under true Ram Raj, man wouldn't be able to oppress even himself. Injustice against oneself is as great a sin as injustice against another. Today, Lord Ram has again thrown Sita out of his house, just because she was compelled to live with Ravan for some time. But was she to blame for it? Wasn't she a victim of deceit and trickery, like our numberless mothers and sisters today? Was it a question of Sita's truth or falsehood? Or of the stark beastliness of the demon Ravan, who has ten human heads, but also has another, bigger one, that of a donkey. Today, our Sita has been expelled once again, totally without fault, our Sita...Laajwanti...' He broke down and wept.

Rasaloo and Neki Ram raised the red banners on which the school children had that very day skilfully cut out and pasted different slogans for them, and the procession got going once again, all shouting 'Long Live Sundar Lal Babu!' in unison. Then someone yelled 'Long Live Sita—the Queen of Virtue!' and someone else 'Shri Ramchandar…'

'Silence! Silence!' a joint cry went up. Within seconds, months of Narain Bawa's labour went down the drain, as a good portion of his congregation got up and joined the procession, led by barrister Kalka Parshad and Hukm Singh, the petition writer at Chauki Kalan, both triumphantly tapping their old walking sticks on the ground. Sundar Lal walked along with them. Tears were still streaming down his cheeks. His heart had been hurt very badly today. The people were shouting with great gusto:

*Touch the leaves of the laajwanti,*
*they curl and wither away.*

The song was still reverberating in the ears of the people. The sun had not yet risen and the widow in house number 414 in Mulla Shakur was still tossing restlessly in her bed. Just then Lal Chand, who was from Sundar Lal's village and whom the latter and Kalka Parshad, using their influence, had helped to set up a ration shop, rushed over to Sundar Lal's. He offered his hand from under his thick, coarse shawl and said, 'Congratulations, Sundar Lal!'

'Congratulations for what, Lal Chand?' Sundar Lal asked, putting some molasses-sweetened tobacco in his chillum.

'I just saw Laaju Bhabhi.'

The chillum fell from Sundar Lal's hand and the tobacco scattered on the floor. 'Where!?' he asked, grabbing Lal Chand by the shoulder, and shaking him hard when he didn't answer quickly enough.

'At the Wagah border.'

He abruptly let go of Lal Chand's shoulder. 'Must be someone else.'

'No, Bhaiya, it really was Laaju,' Lal Chand tried to convince him. 'She was Laaju all right.'

'Do you even know her?' Sundar Lal asked as he gathered the tobacco and ground it between his palms. 'Well then,' he said, removing the chillum from Rasaloo's hookah, 'tell me, what are her distinguishing marks?'

'A tattoo on her chin, another on her cheek.'

'Yes, yes, yes!' Sundar Lal himself completed the description. 'And a third one on her forehead.' He didn't want there to be any doubt.

Suddenly he recalled all those tattoos on Laajwanti's body he had known so well, tattoos she had gotten as a little girl, which resembled the light green spots on the touch-me-not plant and caused it to curl up its leaves at the slightest hint of an approaching hand. Exactly the same way, Laajwanti would curl up from modesty the instant anyone pointed at her tattoos. She would withdraw into herself and disappear, afraid that all her secrets had been let out, that she had been made poor by the plunder of a hidden treasure. And Sundar Lal's entire body began to burn with an unknown fear, with an unknown spirit and its purified fire. He grabbed Lal Chand by the shoulder once again and asked, 'How did Laaju get to Wagah?'

'There was an exchange of abducted women between India and Pakistan,' Lal Chand said.

'What happened then?' Sundar Lal asked, as he squatted down on the floor. 'Tell me, what happened then?'

Rasaloo too sat up in his cot and asked, coughing as only smokers do, 'Is it really true? Laajwanti Bhabhi's returned?'

Lal Chand continued. 'At the Wagah border, Pakistan handed over sixteen women and received sixteen in exchange. But an altercation developed. Our volunteers objected that there were too many middle-aged, old, and useless women in the contingent Pakistan was handing over. A crowd quickly gathered on the scene. Just then, volunteers from the other side pointed at Laaju Bhabhi and said, "Here, you call her old? Have a look. None of the girls you have returned can match her." Meanwhile Laaju Bhabhi was frantically trying to hide her tattoos from the people's probing eyes. The argument got more heated. Each side decided to take back their 'goods'. I cried out, "Laaju! Laaju Bhabhi!" But our own military guards beat us up and drove us away for making a racket.'

Lal Chand bared his elbow to show where he had been struck by a lathi. Rasaloo and Neki Ram remained silent, while Sundar Lal gazed far away into space. Perhaps he was thinking about Laaju, who had returned, but then again had not. He looked like someone who had just crossed the scorching sands of Bikaner and now sat panting under the shade of a tree, his parched tongue hanging out, too exhausted even to ask for water. The realization struck him that the violence of the pre-Partition days still continued even after Partition, only in a different form. Today, people didn't even feel sympathy for the victims. If you asked someone about, say, Lahna Singh and his sister-in-law, Bantu, who used to live in Sambharwala, quick and curt would come the answer: 'Dead!' and the fellow would move on, unaware of death and the difference it made.

Worse still, there were cold-blooded people who traded in human merchandise, in human flesh. Just as at cattle fairs prospective buyers pull back the snout of a cow or a water buffalo to assess its age by examining its teeth, these human traders now put up for public display the beauty of a young woman, her blossoming charm, her most intimate secrets, her beauty spots, her tattoos. This sort of violence had sunk right down to their very bones. In former times, at least, deals were struck at fairs under the protective cover of a handkerchief. Fingers met, negotiated, and concluded in secrecy. Today, however, even that screen had been lifted. Everybody was bargaining shamelessly in the open, with no regard for decorum. This transaction, this peddling, recalled an episode straight out of Boccaccio—a narrative depicting the uninhibited trafficking of women: countless women stand lined up, baring themselves before the Uzbek procurer, who pokes and prods them with his finger. It leaves a pink indentation where it touches the body, a pale circle forms around it, and the pink and the pale rush to meet. The Uzbek moves on, and the rejected woman, crushed by humiliation and shame, sobs uncontrollably, holding the waistcord of her loosened lower garment with one hand, hiding her face from the public's gaze with the other. Later, even the feeling of shame departs. Thus she walks nude through the bazaars of Alexandria. [...]

Sundar Lal was getting ready to go to the border town of Amritsar when the news of Laaju's arrival overtook him. Its suddenness unnerved him. He hurriedly took a step towards the door but, just as swiftly, stepped back. A sudden feeling to give in to his unhappiness overwhelmed him. He felt he wanted to spread all the placards, all the banners of his Rehabilitation Committee out on the floor, and sit on them and cry his heart out. But the situation was hardly proper for such an expression of emotion. He bravely fought back the turmoil raging inside him and picked his way slowly towards Chauki Kalan, the venue for the delivery of the abducted women.

Laaju stood straight in front of him, shaking with fear. If anyone knew Sundar Lal, it was she. She had forgotten none of how badly he had treated her before, and now that she was returning after living with another man, there was no telling what he might do. Sundar Lal looked at Laaju. She had draped the upper half of her body in a black dupatta, one of its ends thrown over her left shoulder in the typical Muslim fashion, but only out of habit. Perhaps it made it easier to socialize with the Muslim ladies and finally to make her escape from her captor. Then again, she had been thinking of Sundar Lal so much and was so mortally afraid of him that she scarcely had the mind to change into different clothes or even to worry about draping herself with the dupatta in the right fashion. As it was, she was unable to distinguish the basic difference between Hindu and

Muslim cultures—whether the dupatta went over the right or left shoulder. Right now, she stood before Sundar Lal, trembling, balanced between hope and fear.

Sundar Lal was shocked. He noticed that Laajwanti looked fairer and healthier than before; indeed she looked plump. Whatever he had imagined about her turned out to be wrong. He had thought that grief would have wasted her, that she'd be too weak even to speak. The thought that she had been happy in Pakistan wounded him, but he said nothing to her, for he had sworn not to quiz her about such matters. All the same, he couldn't help wondering: why had she chosen to return if she lived a happier life there? Perhaps the Indian government had forced her to, against her wishes.

But he was quite unable to see the pallor on Laajwanti's tawny face, or to fathom that it was suffering, and suffering alone, that made her firm flesh loosen and sag from her bones, making her look heavy. She had become heavy with an excess of grief, though superficially she appeared healthy. Hers was the kind of plumpness which made one pant for breath after taking only a few steps.

Sundar Lal's initial gaze at the abducted wife unsettled him. But he fought all his thoughts back with great manliness. Many other people were also present and one of them shouted, 'We're not about to take back these Muslim leavings!'

But the slogans of Rasaloo, Neki Ram, and the old petition writer of Chauki Kalan drowned out the man's voice. Above them all rose the loud, cracking voice of Kalka Parshad, who somehow managed to speak and cough at the same time. He was absolutely convinced of this new reality, this new purity. It seemed he had learnt a new Veda, a new Purana, a new Shastra, which he desperately wanted to share with others. And surrounded by all these people and voices, Laaju and Sundar Lal returned home. It seemed that after a protracted moral exile, the Ramchandar and Sita of an age long past were entering Ayodhya, while the people both celebrated their return by lighting lamps of joy and, at the same time, showed regret for having put the couple through such incredible misery.

Sundar Lal continued his 'Rehabilitation of Hearts' campaign with the same ardour even after Laajwanti's return. He had lived up to it both in word and deed. People who had earlier taken his involvement for just so much sentimental idealism were now convinced of his sincerity. Some were truly happy at this, but most felt disappointed and sad, and many women of the Mulla Shakur neighbourhood, except for the widow, still felt uncomfortable crossing Sundar Lal's threshold.

To Sundar Lal, however, it made no difference at all whether people recognized or ignored his work. The queen of his heart had returned and the yawning emptiness in his chest had been filled. He had installed the golden image of Laaju in the temple of his heart and diligently stood guard at its doorway. Laaju, who used to be so afraid of him, now began slowly to relax under his unexpectedly gentle and caring regard.

Sundar Lal no longer called her Laaju, but 'Devi', which made her go mad with indescribable joy. How much she wanted to tell him what she had been through, and cry so profusely that the tears would wash away all her 'sins', but Sundar Lal deftly avoided listening to her. And so she still carried a trace of apprehension in her new-found ease. After he had fallen asleep, she would simply gaze at him. If he caught her watching him and asked for a reason, she wouldn't know what to say beyond 'Nothing' or 'I don't know'. Sundar Lal, exhausted from the day's gruelling work, would go back to sleep. Once, though, in the beginning, he did ask Laajwanti about her 'dark days'. 'Who was he?'

'His name was Jumma,' she said, with downcast eyes. Then, fixing her eyes on his face, she wanted to say something more, but faltered. He was looking at her in a strange way, as his hands caressed her hair. She lowered her eyes again. Sundar Lal asked, 'Was he good to you?'

'Yes.'

'He didn't beat you?'

'No,' Laajwanti said, dropping her head on Sundar Lal's chest. 'He never hurt me. And yet I was very afraid of him. You used to beat me, but I never felt scared of you. You won't beat me again, ever, will you?'

Tears welled up in Sundar Lal's eyes. He said, feeling deep shame and regret, 'No, never again, Devi.'

'Devi!' Laajwanti thought, and she too broke down in tears.

She felt overwhelmed by a desire to tell him all, holding back nothing, but Sundar Lal stopped her saying, 'Let's just forget the past. You were hardly to blame for what happened. Society is at fault for its lack of respect for goddesses like you. In that it doesn't harm you a bit, only itself.'

And Laajwanti couldn't get it all out. It remained buried inside her. She withdrew into herself and stared at her body for the longest time, a body which, after the Partition of the country, was no longer hers, but that of a goddess. Yes, she was happy, indeed very happy, but it was a happiness marred by a nagging doubt, a misgiving. She would sit up in bed with a start, like someone surrounded by a surfeit of happiness who suddenly hears an approaching sound and looks apprehensively in its direction, waiting.

Ultimately, the nagging doubt replaced happiness with a chilling finality. And not because Sundar Lal Babu had again started mistreating her, but because he had started treating her with exceeding gentleness. She didn't expect that from him. She wanted to be the same old Laaju once again, the one who would quarrel over trifles and then make up in no time at all. Now, though, there was no possibility of even a quarrel. Sundar Lal had convinced her that she was in fact a laajwanti, a glass object too fragile to withstand the merest touch. Laaju would look at herself in the mirror, and after thinking long and hard would feel that she could be many things, but could never hope to be the old Laaju ever again. Yes, she had been rehabilitated, but she had also been ruined. Sundar Lal, on his part, had neither the eyes to see her tears, nor the ears to hear her painful groans. How fragile the human heart can be—this escaped even the most ardent reformer of the Mulla Shakur neighbourhood. The early morning processions continued and, like a robot, he joined in the refrain with Rasaloo and Neki Ram:

*Touch the leaves of the laajwanti,*
*they curl and wither away.*

five

~

# TAJ*

## TIMERI N. MURARI

I, Prince Shah Jahan, no longer the boy named Khurrum, but Sovereign of the World and heir to the Emperor Jahangir, Padishah of Hindustan, though still only fifteen, strutting in the mantle as my father's favourite son, had been invited to attend the Royal Meena Bazaar. I had trembled with the excitement of the event, for my presence was a sign of the favour not only of my father but also of the court. They all adjudged me to be the heir to this vast empire, over my three brothers. To rule, to hold the sceptre of power, can be the only ambition of a young prince. On this night, I felt the bazaar would be a fortuitous event.

The Royal Meena Bazaar had been established by my great-grandfather, Emperor Humayun. It was a delightful idea for, by imperial decree, the women could appear unveiled in front of a chosen audience of men.

*Extracted from *Taj: A Story of Mughal India*

The silken masks worn all year round were, for a single evening, discarded. The narrow world of the haram was to be turned inside out; for a few brief hours we would gaze on the naked faces of the noble ladies.

In spite of the heat and the stillness of the air, it seemed a current flowed through the palace as the evening approached. Stalls had been erected by the workmen in the garden and, doubtless, the women had chosen the wares they would offer for sale. I had heard they bargained and haggled like the women in the street chowk, and that the buyer purchased, if he were lucky, not only the wares, but the favours of the lady herself. I had heard nobles, a favoured few, boast about their conquests, sigh longingly of the pleasurable nights spent with a lady. I too was not inexperienced in these matters. I had lain with my slave girls and sometimes, for amusement, had gone with companions to the dancers in the bazaars and paid for their bodies. But I had learnt through experience that, because of my position, I could expect only fleshly pleasure from women. I did not listen to their whispers, for they whispered only to flatter me, to gain favours and wealth. The poets wrote and sang of love, of men and women wasting and dying from this strange sickness, but to me love was an illusion; the palace a desert of affection.

As I was bathed and dressed I smiled with anticipation and, seeing this, the slave girls teased me about the evening: I would meet a princess, oh yes. It had been forecast by the astrologer that the prince would be lucky. He would fall in love and live forever in happiness. I laughed at their teasing and did not believe them. And yet, I wondered: why was I excited? Was it the thought of seeing the faces of women I had glimpsed, heard speak, but never boldly looked upon?

The pleasurable game of matching voice to face, hands to face, eyes to face. What else could I look forward to: a night or two of pleasure, possibly a week, a month? I found this prospect tedious. I could choose any girl in this chamber to sate my lust.

Yet, the air felt as if thunder waited. Was it a sense of dread?

Two companions joined me, the Nawab of Ajmer and a nobleman, Allami Sa'du-lla Khan. They were dressed as splendidly as I and, though older, appeared to be just as anxious and excited. They too had never attended a Royal Bazaar. They went to the balcony, looked out over the garden; it was ablaze with lights, candles flickered in every niche, lanterns were hanging from the trees and stalls, and were caught and reflected in the waters of the fountain. They saw the shadows and heard the laughter.

'We must hurry, we must go.'

'Wait awhile,' I ordered. 'Drink some wine, pause and savour the pleasures to come.'

They obeyed, but only because I spoke. They did not recline, but hung over the balcony gazing greedily down, as if the fools had never seen women before. I wanted their company to pass the time, to talk of hunting and our sports.

'Sit!'

They sat, restive, straining like cheetahs. I felt no different, but a prince must always show control, otherwise he is powerless. But I lost their attention when we heard the dundhubi beating the approach of my father, Jahangir. From the balcony, we saw him enter the garden, trailed by a serpent of courtiers.

For a moment, all fell silent, all paid homage, and then the chattering and the music continued.

'Wait a few minutes longer, until my father is occupied.'

When I judged that the frenzy had abated, and that the emperor would not be a distraction from my own entrance, we went down.

It was truly a bazaar; perfumed women squatted in their stalls in front of mounds of silk, cases of jewellery fashioned in gold and silver, toys, perfumes, ivory carvings, little marble statues. The air was sweet with their voices and laughter, and the soft sounds of music. My presence was immediately acknowledged and the women by the entrance laughed and clapped. Their eyes were bold and inviting, each calling to me to buy from her stall alone, some tugging at my sleeves like the chokras in a real bazaar. See my wares, sample this; it is cheap, especially for Shah Jahan. Look at this silk…here is a vase from Bengal. Their very lives could have depended on the sale, such was their enthusiasm. I strolled through the lanes, noting the faces and bodies, some pretty, others not, old and young, thin and fat. They were all boisterous, bawdy, like birds set free from their cages, wheeling and chirping in the garden. Their chattering was incessant, a torment to me, and it was by chance, to avoid a persistent lady, that I turned away.

How can I explain the sudden helplessness, the suffocation of all my senses? She knelt in the lane beyond, quiet and alone, remote from the tamasha. True, it was her beauty, a perfect oval face, large eyes, a mouth like a budding rose and, in her shining black hair, a single strand of jasmine, that caught my eye, but it was her serenity that held me. She looked this way and that, seeing everything, and all with great amusement. A smile rose gently to her face, from within, quite unlike the shallow laughter of the other women. I saw what no other possessed: honesty. I felt that if I spoke, she would listen to me, and not hear the prince. My heart, my heart, it pained with beating, and when she turned and saw me through the opening, it stopped. I was truly afraid—and not even all the might I could command in this world could control the burst of fear—that she would turn away from me. I sensed immediately that any disinterest in her would not arise from flirtation, but from true indifference. Suddenly, I was no longer afraid. She remained still, looking at me, curious, amused and—what is it?—I felt as if we touched.

I cannot recall how I reached her side. I was there, and saw that her stall sold silver jewellery, a small and humble offering, and that she was assisted by a chokra. I could not contain myself; I was bursting with words and feelings.

'I felt as if we touched.' I spoke loudly, swiftly, unable to control the authority of my tongue which was more used to commanding than to revealing my heart. I tried again. 'But it was not possible at that distance. Yet I felt your arm gently on mine. To love swiftly is to chance life itself. It is a leap of trust, like entering a battle without the protection of armour, believing that somehow you cannot be killed. But even if you were killed, mere existence would not be worth it without you. You must tell me who you are. I must hear your voice and know you are truly real and not a dream that will disappear like water in this heat.'

'Arjumand Banu, your highness.'

Her voice was incense, soft, sweetly rising in the air. Unsettled by my intense stare, she lowered her eyes in modesty and began to bow in obeisance. It was enough to cause my heart to ache and I reached swiftly to stop her, touching her bare shoulder. I felt as if I had been struck.

'Your skin burns me, and causes my heart to beat like the drum of war.'

'Your highness only tells me what I already feel.' It seemed then she slanted her head and brushed the back of my hand with her cheek. 'It is possibly the heat in the air.'

'No, no. That only strikes our surface, causing us some little discomfort. This enters deep into the flesh, simmering my heart, muddling my mind. I do not even know of what I speak.'

'The words are sweet, your highness,' she moved gently, and my hand fell away. I still felt the seductive softness of her cheek, like a brand pressed into my skin. 'Your tongue is too practised to stumble at the sight of a girl.'

'Here,' I snatched my dagger out. 'It if lies, cut it out. I cannot help its sweetness. It curls through the feelings in my heart and the only sound I can hear in my head is the blood repeating: "Arjumand… Arjumand." Did you not feel the same when we first looked on each other?'

'Yes, your highness. But it feels as if I have returned to sleep and entered the dream…'

'What dream?'

'I cannot tell it all. But when I awoke this morning, I felt as I did when I first saw you here'. She searched my face carefully, seeing beyond skin and bone, gazing through my own eyes at what lay inside: 'You are real. This isn't still the dream.'

I knelt down in front of her, as she too knelt in her stall, and eagerly put out my hand for her touch.

'Feel the fever of my body again. You're awake, like me.'

Shyly she touched my hand, and once more we sensed in each the shock. It seemed the lightning that lit the skies in the monsoons leaped between us. I wished us to remain touching, but she withdrew, convinced now we were together and not separate in different dreams.

'I will sit here forever and look on you.'

She laughed, and the gentle sound made me feel as if I were tumbling through the notes of some strange and lovely music.

'We will grow old then, just staring at one another.'

'What better life could we have? I wish it were day, with the sun full on you. These shadows cheat me. They bend your nose, and yet it is perfect. They darken your eyes, and yet I know they are clear and beautiful. But even they cannot change the shape of your mouth or the curve of your cheek.'

'Do you only see so little of me? There are countless others in this palace who far surpass my beauty.'

'No. None can do that. What they reveal lies only on the surface. I see beyond your eyes and your face. I feel that I have known you all my life, and yet I know nothing. I cannot help but thank god that I saw you on this evening.'

'Yes,' and her voice fell to wonder. 'But I could have looked on you, day upon day, year upon year, and you would never have dreamt of my existence.'

'But I would have, I would have,' I said eagerly, wishing to persuade her. 'It isn't only the sight of each other that has drawn us together. Don't you feel it is beyond sight, beyond touch, beyond hearing? I felt your touch in my heart over distance, as you felt mine. Even through the veil I would have known your love. It is so, isn't it?'

'It cannot be anything other, your highness.'

I wished she had not spoken those words. I felt a tremor, a vibration that started to shred the fabric of my feeling.

'If I was not a prince…' I began.

'If you were less, I could not feel less.'

I looked into her eyes. They were wide, unflinching, allowing me to see behind the words she spoke. I felt the tremor cease, and could not disguise my joy. I laughed out loud, and heard her whisper: 'But how do I address you?'

'My love, my delight. You are my chosen one, my love.'

'My love,' she spoke in a whisper, delighting my whole being, suffusing me with longing to hold her.

We knelt still, looking on each other, not wishing to miss a glance, a smile, a gesture. We could not tear our gaze away.

Who knows how much time we passed in this manner. I could not have cared even if it had been a lifetime. I felt a touch on my shoulder, breaking the soft silence of our world, and looked up in annoyance. Allami Sa'du-lla Khan bowed apologetically, and seeing the swift flash of anger, merely gestured around. The crowd gathering around were barely silent, staring at us.

'Let them. I am Shah Jahan. Now withdraw.'

'Your highness, you should be seen elsewhere too. The women ask where is Shah Jahan so we may bless him. You cannot ignore their wishes.'

'I will come soon. Withdraw.' He drew away, and I returned to my love. 'I will talk to my father about us.'

She bowed in acceptance. 'If it is his will…'

'It is mine,' I spoke firmly, and rose to my feet. She remained kneeling, but her face lifted to continue looking on mine. I wished then to swiftly bend and touch my lips to hers, but I did not. She knew what I wished and smiled mischievously.

'There will be other times when we will not have to endure

so many watching eyes.' From her stall, she picked up a piece of silver. 'Will not my love buy a memento? Having spent so much time, you cannot leave empty-handed, and I should at least have a rupee or two.'

'And what will you do with a rupee?'

'Give it to the poor. They have more need than we do.'

'The poor.' I could not hide my surprise.

'Hasn't my love noticed them? They live outside this palace.'

'When I am with you, I notice very little else. The world ceases its existence, and only we two live. If it is for the poor then, I will buy everything. How much?'

She frowned and studied her pile of silver jewellery, and then glancing up, gave me a smile full of fun.

'Ten thousand rupees.'

'I have a bargain.'

She began to laugh, peeking at me through the curtain of hair that fell over her face. I could not bear such happiness and wished like a thief to steal and ride away with her. Instead, I turned to my slave and placed the bag of money he carried on the floor of her tiny stall.

'I will see you again.'

'If it is your wish.'

six

~

# DESOLATION, LUST

## UPAMANYU CHATTERJEE

The slow train stopped yet again. Atri had read in a plaintive article somewhere that in the suburbs, many commuters, when near their houses, pulled the alarm chains to stop the trains. Then they scuttled across the tracks to their hovels in grey concrete blocks. Beyond the train window, two feet away, stood a sheet of corrugated iron. A hole had been torn in it. The back of a mirror at the base of the hole, around the mirror a man's sagging etiolated chest, with nipples dark pink, like suppurative insect bites. A bit of his right arm moved rhythmically beside the mirror. He was shaving. Here by the tracks, sharing an iron box with the rats of Bombay, surrounded by defecation, it was absurd, it seemed to Atri, that this man was shaving. With his smooth cheeks and chin, he must keep up appearances; Atri half-smiled at that thought. Once that man must've been new to the city, long before it made him its denizen. Work might've wrenched him away from home too, and dumped him here, one more inhabitant of one more city of encroachments and unauthorized constructions, where his glimpses of the sun were dependent on his shaving mirror and the unscheduled halts of trains. The train started again, but the desolation remained.

Atri felt completely empty and remote. He looked down at the dried mudprints of slippers on the compartment floor. This arrival in an alien unknown place was inevitable, like birth or death, this weaning away from home, inescapable, a second severed umbilical cord. He leaned his head against the window stains and watched the passing poles and wires and blocks of concrete. There is not a blade of grass in Bombay, Anand had said. Except the scrub rising out of the excrement by the tracks. God, the agonies one suffered just to stay sad and half-alive. Again Atri half-smiled at his self-pity.

Across from him, Sheela uncrossed her legs and continued to stare out. Atri looked at her gross, seductive face. Abruptly she said, 'Pultu, you should know something.' Atri hated his pet name but Sheela thought it cute. 'I might be pregnant.' The train was slowing down again. She looked at him a little tensely, as though prepared for almost any reaction.

How can anyone called Pultu make a girl pregnant, thought Atri fleetingly. 'You're sure?'

'I think so. I'm always regular, now I'm ten days overdue.'

Like a library book, thought Atri's disordered mind. They watched the train move into the pandemonium of Bombay Central. Hot coolies with large sweat patches and loud voices surged through the train. Atri and Sheela got off. He saw the queues at the ticket counter and the anxious, unseeing railway-station faces and still wanted a ticket home. Outside they battled the rabble of hotel- and taxi-pimps. In the cab Atri said loudly, to beat the million horns, 'Have you done anything about this?'

'I thought you should know first.' Atri looked at her, her profile, at the dandruff in her hair. He patted Sheela's thigh and said, 'I'm sure everything'll be okay.' She nodded. The taxi turned into a gate. 'That wasn't long,' said Atri.

The Training Institute was shabby and one-storeyed. There was green slime on some of the many damp patches on the walls and an iron grille instead of a door into the lobby. A faint smell of dead rats and smegma which, in later years, Atri would always associate with Bombay. Just behind the grille sat a thin, genial man in an office chair, happily and loudly sucking in his tea from a saucer. 'I'll need help with my luggage,' said Atri.

'Oye Chhotu!' yelled the man into the corridor behind the water cooler. He turned back to Atri. 'You've come for the training sir?'

Atri and the taxi man took his luggage off. Sheela remained in the back seat. 'Don't know how long settling in will take. I'll come over as soon as I'm free. Should I telephone first?'

'It's just here.' Sheela gestured over her head. 'On Marine Drive itself. A lovely flat, you can almost walk it from here.' Atri looked at her wide purple lips and heavy jowls. They nodded and smiled awkwardly at each other. The taxi left. Atri remembered the June afternoon when he had suggested that they bathe together. Sheela had been shy and reluctant beneath her flippancy. Her banter had irritated him. Even when he had desired her he had felt alone.

Chhotu was sitting on Atri's blue suitcase. He was a small, powerful man. 'Where's the office?' asked Atri. In reply Chhotu pushed his chin out towards the grille. He, the thin man and Atri shared the luggage. The thin man talked a lot. The hostel room was instantly depressing. A broken cement floor, with small craters. Atri stumbled over one. Old pink walls, two windows. One looked out on to a small field where some urchins played at cricket with a stick and an indistinguishable grey blob for a ball. Behind the field the rest of the universe was stopped by the nether floors of a skyscraper. Countless air-conditioners and some jagged holes in windowpanes. Beyond the other window

Atri saw a bare narrow patch, a wire fence, then some sweating men in loincloths. 'Who are they?'

'The Youth Club, sir. People come for exercise,' said the thin man.

'This room's dirty. Can you arrange for a sweeper?'

Atri followed the thin man out and asked for the office. The open corridor looked on to a big cement courtyard. On the cement were the fading lines of a badminton court. The office lay beyond the courtyard. Its first room had an old desk and behind it a short, fat, bald, bespectacled and extremely unhelpful man. His breath seemed somehow to smell of farts. Atri said, 'What are the joining formalities? I have to sign in.'

Looking down on the bald head with its strands sprouting up above the left ear and stretching heroically across to the right, Atri wondered at himself. Here, in a strange building, in an unknown city, alone, signing up for a job I'm not interested in, having made a girl pregnant, what am I doing? He wanted to peel off the bald man's strands and let them hang beside his ear. They could reach, thought Atri, the pens in the shirt pocket, or they could gag his mouth and lessen its stench. In this daze Atri met the Director of the Institute and then returned to his room.

While settling in he thought disconnectedly of home and Sheela. In his dislocation he remembered the afternoon when, to lunch-hour music from the radio, he had taught Sheela how to inhale smoke. Earlier she used to puff away at cigarettes without inhaling. How dizzy and sick she had felt.

At lunch Atri met a Mrs Karve, the other trainee. 'Normally a batch of three or four, but this year you are small, just the two of you,' smiled the Director. Mrs Karve was from some obscure Maharashtrian town. She had two children. Atri was immediately prepared to be disinterested in her. She was short and a little squat. Mr Karve was something in the State Bank.

In the late afternoon, before leaving to meet Sheela, Atri

wrote a letter home. For a moment, he was tempted to write, 'Ma, Sheela is pregnant. Maybe she's lying to get me to marry her.' Sheela was staying with her sister and brother-in-law in a huge, old flat on Marine Drive. According to Sheela her brother-in-law had often been offered unimaginable prices for it. She used to talk often of her holidays in Bombay.

Her sister Alka seemed friendly. 'I can't believe this is your first visit to Bombay. I mean, *everyone* has been to Bombay.'

'He's absolutely rural, yaar,' laughed Sheela. Atri was surprised at what he took to be her false gaiety. Compared to her sister's, Sheela's voice was even more loud and jarring.

Alka left for the kitchen to organize coffee. Atri moved out to the verandah. Sheela followed. The bright sun on a sea of rippled glass, the sea endless and oblivious, and below the distant toys bustling on Marine Drive. 'Your sister's very pretty,' said Atri.

'It runs in the family,' smiled Sheela.

On the breeze drifted in the nauseating smell of the sea. At last Atri said, 'You have to get an abortion, no?'

'Let's discuss that later.'

Atri was surprised. He moved closer, but she pulled away. 'We've never discussed marriage but this shouldn't force us into it.'

'Later.' Sheela was loud all evening. She played raucously with her nephew, an eight-month-old bore who resembled Winston Churchill. He urinated on her and she pressed her face into his stomach. Atri was by turns bored, irritated and worried. 'How dull you are not to like children,' said Sheela. Atri wondered whether she had told her sister about her pregnancy. Satish the brother-in-law arrived, short, soft and fat, something in some ad agency. His spectacles were tinted and he looked like a maker of hard porn. He fixed Atri a whisky. They pulled chairs out to the verandah and watched Sheela change the piddler's nappy. 'You married?' asked Satish.

'No.'

Satish nodded several times. Atri stayed to dinner. While Sheela distracted the child, he helped Alka lay the table. He noticed the thin, wrinkled skin on the back of Alka's hands, it looked almost brittle. He wouldn't have associated that skin with the moist, adhesive heat of Bombay.

'Sheela's good with the child.'

'Yeah, she's too stupid to be anything more in life than an ayah,' laughed Alka. The two sisters got on well and seemed to like each other.

Sheela drove him back in the Maruti. 'You drive very badly. You're really rash and blind,' said Atri.

'But I love driving. With my father I never get to touch the car. Here with my sister I can do what I like and Satish is very nice. He taught me driving when I was here four years ago. My parents are boring, yaar, compared to my sister.' Sheela talked on, unnecessarily. Atri had often told her that she spoke so loudly because she was a little deaf, and that was because she always listened to her cassettes on the headphones of her Walkman. At the pizza parlour near her hostel, she had as usual closed her eyes and begun nodding her head to the monotonous rock music. Then Micky had picked up the Walkman and whispered into it. Her beatific smiles had then turned genuine. Later Micky had said, 'I said some sexy stuff into that stupid machine. She wants it bad. I'll hump her, you joker, before you even get close enough to smell her skin.'

'When should we discuss the pregnancy?' Atri interrupted Sheela.

She said nothing, but took a right turn at great speed. Atri also kept quiet. His sense of desolation made him passive, quiescent in front of any outrage or complication that might involve him.

At the gate of the Training Institute Sheela asked, 'Coming home tomorrow?'

Atri poked his head in through the window. 'What about your pregnancy?' The word sounded alien.

'So?' Sheela's tone was aggressive, though she was looking away.

'We've to get a pregnancy test. Do you know anyone in Bombay?'

'No.'

'Should we tell your sister?'

'No.'

Atri got back into the car, reluctantly prepared for a long discussion. 'We'll have to return to Delhi as soon as we can.' Any reason, he thought, to get home.

Sheela said nothing. The silence was faintly hostile. Atri returned to his room and wrote a letter to a friend in Delhi. 'Anand, an emergency. Send me a telegram saying, Ma in hospital after a heart attack. Come. Sign it Papa. No jokes. Send it immediately, and Lightning. I'll explain why when we meet. Otherwise things are okay. This place promises to be really dull, maybe Madras and Jabalpur'll be better. I'm training with a female called Karve. But send the telegram.'

Atri went out right then, at midnight, to post the letter at the box by the gate. His letter of appointment to the job had said unequivocally that leave during training was impossible.

The cement courtyard was brightly moonlit. The surrounding corridors were black and faintly menacing. Atri could hear the distant, eternal noise of the city. The corridors and courtyard reminded him of some ancient ancestral house, perhaps in Lucknow, where a huge, unmanageable, impoverished family would have lived and quarrelled together.

The fake telegram was an old and trusted ploy, but Atri wasn't particularly interested in its success. Nothing seemed to matter. He returned to his room, switched off the light and got into bed. With the darkness came desire. Once, just seven months ago, on an impulse, he had sent a telegram to Sheela at her hostel. The telegram had merely read, 'I lust you very much'. To Atri the act had been exhilarating. Sheela had been both touched and embarrassed. For in the hostel all telegrams were put up on the Mess Notice Board, open, their secrets unprotected. Everyone had read his message. It had then seemed silly.

He tried to explain to Sheela once how he felt, that love was a euphemism, that what everyone felt and eulogized was actually lust and the sense of possession. There were these phases in one's life, late teenage, or the middle twenties, when one expected of oneself to fall in love, when one was expected to be seen with a girl, attending seminars, catching buses, seeing movies in large outwardly happy groups. But lust was different, and not as transient. It was a biological necessity, like a part of one's metabolism. Then the personality and wishes of the object of lust didn't matter, and lust was somehow linked with the loneliness, which was infinitely more fundamental and long-lasting. Sheela had been offended, hadn't shown it, but had scoffed at his theorizing. She had said, 'You think it's very, what's the word, macho? To say you feel lust and no love and all that rubbish, because admitting to love you think will be sentimental.' Atri had had no wish to explain further because he had a core he found impossible to unveil. But he had disliked her for her assurance and the confidence with which she claimed him. I'm precious too, he had wanted to tell her, and I want to be alone and free; he had seen her as a threat to his dreams of dispossession.

He woke to the clink of metal. The room looked less ugly in the soft early-morning light. On the wall a patch of yellow showed up where the caked pink limewash had fallen off. The patch was shaped vaguely like Australia. Atri watched it unthinkingly.

The sounds were from the Youth Club beyond the window. After a while someone hammered at the door. Tea. Atri went over to the window. The tea was hot, sweet and sickening. A few feet away stood a sweating torso on pale, trembling pencil legs. With his mind elsewhere Atri watched the disproportionate figure tug at a barbell.

At Lucknow station, over a year ago, Atri had seen Sheela perfectly, it seemed to him, the oval head jigging with laughter at Micky's joke, surrounded by suitcases, leaning against a pillar proclaiming a new Hindi film. Dipping his stale rusk in his tea, with the roar of the chaiwala's gas stove in his ears, Atri had remembered then that Micky had said, she's from Calcutta, yaar, all these Cal females are as loose as pyjamas, you can make her anytime. In the following months the confused Atri had often felt that if Sheela had been more affected, less open and friendly somehow, then he would have apologized for the grossness of his emotions.

At breakfast Atri sat beside Mrs Karve. Her sari was an eye-blinding green. 'It's sad that there are only two of us. If there had been more, then we could've written letters in class without their ever noticing us.'

Mrs Karve smiled politely. 'You're from Delhi?' Her Maharashtrian accent was strong.

'Yes.' Pause. 'How old are your children?'

'Dattatreya is five and Dinkar will be three this month. I am going to miss his birthday.'

'Tch tch.' They laughed at that.

The introductory lectures were excruciating. Before leaving for Bombay, Atri had heard his father yet again on marriage and loneliness. 'I didn't want to marry your mother, Pultu, you know that. On the day of the marriage, in the taxi in Egmore, but you have no idea of Madras, we were going to the Registry Office, I said to her in the taxi, we shouldn't marry because I'm not the right person to marry. That wasn't an original line, or even an original thought, it must've been said a million times before, but I meant it. She didn't like it, of course, how could she? Our marriage hasn't been very happy. I'm still lonely, I suppose so is she.'

After the afternoon session Atri automatically got into a taxi to go to Alka's flat. He didn't particularly want to meet Sheela, but he felt an obscure obligation. He again settled down in an armchair and watched her with her nephew who again wet himself. 'Does he have diabetes, you think? The amount he piddles.' The sisters laughed.

Later he asked Sheela for a walk down Marine Drive. 'Forget it, yaar,' she said, 'feeling too lazy.' Atri was irritated and said, 'I've written to Anand to send a telegram to me. As soon as it comes we should go back to Delhi and work out your pregnancy.' He immediately thought, I should've said the pregnancy, or perhaps our pregnancy.

Sheela said nothing and cooed to the child. Atri went out to the verandah to look at the sea, immense and impersonal. Once he had been excited about Bombay. He had thought of nights with Sheela away from her confining hostel and its Auschwitzean rules. But here with her sister and nephew she was another person. Strange. He had considered himself a successful strategist when she used to lie to her warden and come away with him. Now those once-exquisite assignations in borrowed rooms, the lying together with minds at rest, and gauging the passage of the hours by the glow of the sun on the pink bougainvillea by the window, all that seemed remote, sometimes a little sordid.

Sheela came out. Atri said, 'As soon as I get the telegram I'll ask the Director for leave. Then you say you forgot to submit your exam forms. If you like I'll telephone you from somewhere, and you pretend it's someone from Delhi, a classmate or something, say Raman, who telephoned about the exam forms. And the last date is imminent etcetera so you have to return.' Atri stopped listlessly. 'Why didn't you tell me this in Delhi, before we left?'

'I didn't want to spoil anything. I was scared.'

Atri didn't want to accuse or to hurt, not just then anyway. But he did want to escape the fetters of guilt. Yet away from her there seemed to be only desolation and lust; and with her there wasn't much else. He had always enjoyed being alone, but it seemed to him that Sheela had brought him a kind of emptiness. It couldn't be true, yet the moments of joy now seemed so remote. He picked up a cushion from the verandah floor and threw it on to the rocking chair. The chair began to move. To its creak, Sheela said, 'I'm still scared because I don't know what's going to happen.'

'You were very regular, no?'

'As regular as the bloody moon.'

Atri smiled at her reply and turned to her. But Sheela, with eyes closed, had lifted up her face to the warm sea breeze. He spoke to her profile. 'Maybe it's just delayed or something. But we'll feel more secure in Delhi, won't we? We know people there, we know…the city. Here,' he gestured helplessly at the skyline. Sheela was in her tight orange corduroys. He felt faintly the stirrings of desire. In school they had been made to study a poem called 'My Last Duchess' by Robert Browning. The poem had been about a Duke who kills his wife, or something like that. Atri had liked one bit:

> Oh sir, she smiled, no doubt,
> Whene'er I passed her; but who passed without
> Much the same smile?

In school the lines had seemed to apply to his mother. Later Atri saw Sheela also as absolutely undiscriminating in her friendships; 'at least holding hands with anything in pants', Micky had once said. Atri had thought that his mother and Sheela would hit it off together. After her first visit, Atri's mother had summed up Sheela as cheap and vulgar. 'Lust,' she had said, clinking her bangles while she poured out the tea, 'is making you see her as good company. She has a good body, and a good skin, and a vulgar, attractive face. You two have nothing in common. You're not serious about her, I hope?'

'I've told you so often, Ma, I only want to marry a divorced Muslim transvestite whore.'

'She's probably that too.'

Atri's mother was intermittently inquisitive about Atri. She used to snoop around in his room, and had once unearthed a book called *Your Contraceptions.* As a joke Atri had bought it for

Sheela and had written in it, 'In the years to come, my lust, you are not going to say that I did not have foresight.' His mother had said that the book confirmed her opinion of Sheela.

The shriek of slammed brakes drifted up from Marine Drive. From their verandah, as from an eyrie, they watched the distant tableau. A white Fiat askew, the disturbed traffic, the crowd forming, and in the background, as always, the hush of the uncaring sea. 'We always used condoms. I mean I always did. How did it happen?'

'One must have had a hole in it. Remember that joke about a bastard perforating condoms in revenge.'

'Is it an accident or isn't it?' From that height they couldn't quite make out.

'Which do you mean?' They both laughed, a little startled by the unexpected joy.

The cars began queuing. At the corner, the cleverer drivers, the old hands who knew the traffic snarls of Bombay, were turning off Marine Drive into the street with the ice-cream shop Sheela had raved about the night before. She said, 'How's training?'

'As boring. I sat in class and dreamed about my PhD at MIT.'

'How are the others?' Sheela interrupted him. She had often suffered his dreams of studying at MIT.

'There's only one other. She's okay. Prabha Karve. A mother of many children with unpronounceable names. She's short and has tufts of black hair around her midriff. Not just down, but thick wavy hair.'

'Again you judge by appearances. I've often told you, behind my sexy face lies a heart of gold.'

'Unlikely.' But Sheela did not laugh at that. She looked down at the traffic. Atri felt foolish and continued speaking to cloak his awkwardness. 'Mrs Karve's even been to Jabalpur. She said it's quite a nice place. I said I was petrified of going there for the training later. One more small town in this vast Indian hinterland.

Just Karve and me, it's going to be really boring and lonely.'

'You can always make her pregnant.'

'Bitch.' They laughed.

'You'll get leave?'

'I'll lie, shouldn't be difficult.' Atri paused and moved closer to Sheela. He looked back into the room. Alka wasn't there. He bent down and gently kissed Sheela's shoulder. She shifted a little. 'I like your smell,' he said.

Alka appeared with coffee. They spoke of the weather and the traffic jam. 'How's the training?' she asked Atri.

'Teething troubles, that's this child's problem,' laughed Sheela. 'Can't grow into his new job. He once dreamed of a PhD and now can't wake up. But I think he will soon, poor boy, misses his mama's lap.'

Two days later the telegram arrived while Atri was in a lecture, absentmindedly eyeing Mrs Karve's midriff. It read, 'Ma in uppal with fart attack. Come.' The vulpine Director asked Atri to ring up Delhi from his office. 'We have an STD, go ahead.'

Silently cursing the grace with which the Director cross-checked the telegram, Atri dialled Alka's house, and then dialled three digits at random after the phone began to ring. 'Amazing,' Atri beamed at the Director, his fist holding the receiver, 'got through to Delhi first try.' A woman's voice answered. Atri hoped that it wasn't Alka and began in a high, loud voice.

'Hallo, is that Delhi? Hallo? Is that Papa? Papa, Atri here.'

'What rubbish—'

'Hallo, Papa, I just got the telegram—'

'Oh hi Raman! Hi! What, from Delhi? How did you get my number?'

Atri turned his back to the Director to hide his suppressed giggles. But he couldn't contain the heaving of his stomach. A warmth at Sheela's quick uptake suffused him. 'How serious is it?'

'Oh yes, obviously. You always ring up for some boring reason or other.'

'Oh poor Ma, I'll get leave from here, I'll catch the first available train home.'

'Ohhhh! Of course, how horrible, ohhh now what do I do, huh, Raman, please?'

'No, don't bother about the station, I'll just take a taxi or something.'

'Yes, that's the only thing, but how disgusting of me to forget. Yes, I suppose that'll be the thing to do.'

'Don't worry, Papa, I'm coming.'

'Thanks a lot for calling Raman, you're a real friend, and just tell that bastard Maheshwari I'll get him the forms in time.'

'Okay, Papa, bye, and see you very soon.'

'Yes, I'll do just that, thanks once again, bye, be seeing you soon.'

Atri turned to the Director and said, 'A heart attack, sir. My mother's back home now, but she wants to meet me very much. Thank you, sir, for the phone.'

With one wave, the Director sent Atri's gratitude to the ceiling. 'You should leave as quickly as you can.'

'Thank you, sir. I'll go and check about the tickets.'

Again the taxi for Sheela's. Atri was galled even by this ritual, this meaningless daily seven rupees. The taxi stopped at a light near some massive telecommunications tower. He remembered, ages ago it seemed, the first film that he and Sheela had seen together, an insane Hindi extravaganza in a huge, new hall in Lucknow. They had enjoyed the trash so much just because they had been together, knee touching knee, fingertips occasionally on forearm. She had laughed helplessly when he had breathed into her ear that the vamp in the film looked amazingly like her. Atri remembered fragments of their common past in abrupt flashes, and most of these memories confused him, because their magic seemed irretrievable.

Sheela opened the cream door. Her face glowed with conspiracy. 'I've to return to Delhi immediately. I forgot to fill up those bloody examination forms.' She stank of tobacco and her perfume. He had told her often how much he liked that smell. 'It's much simpler than bathing, yaar,' she had once said.

'You got leave? Talk,' she whispered, and gently patted his stomach.

'Be careful. There's a baby in there.'

'Bastard.' They laughed. Again between them a flicker.

'This stupid girl,' said Alka over tea, 'takes off on a holiday without bothering to find out whether she has to do anything important first.'

'Absolutely right,' said Atri.

'It's just an exam form,' laughed Sheela, 'I can always stay here and fill up my forms next year.'

'I might be going too,' said Atri. 'Three or four holidays coming up, some Marathi hero died or was born or something.' He had always concocted with ease. 'We could go together, but how do we get train tickets?'

'Oh Satish will get that done.'

The globular, lemon-green shade that hung from the ceiling danced in the salt breeze from the windows. 'I think we should leave tomorrow,' said Sheela, 'we'll never get tickets for tomorrow.' Again Atri registered her loud voice. His Second Standard class teacher had always said in class, 'Learn to speak softly. That is good manners.' Atri suddenly wanted to say so to Sheela, to jolt her out of her happiness. Then Churchill started shrieking from the bedroom. 'Time for the bastard's feed,' said Sheela.

Satish proved inquisitive. 'Which Marathi hero? I don't think there is any holiday this week.'

How do people ever plan things like murders with people like Satish around, thought Atri irrationally, and said, 'The Institute is closed for two or three days. Thought it must be a Marathi hero. Never bothered to find out why, just in case it was a mistake and they opened up again.'

A valedictory dinner that night. They all drank a little and laughed a lot. Atri saw Sheela's head jerk back. When she laughed, when her lips split and her belly shook, the sound followed later and sometimes never. She doesn't know the implications of pregnancy, thought Atri, the child.

Two mornings later, again the nondescript ugliness of Bombay Central. Atri watched the insane bustle on the local trains on another platform. The human mass at the mouths of coaches resembled fish eggs. Small, dark, agile men leaped into it with cane baskets and disappeared, like frogs into mud. Their train glided out on time. They waved to Alka and the child. Atri again noticed how much prettier than Sheela she was and felt vaguely guilty. From the window, passing glimpses of Bombay's suburban stations, with their odd, attractive names; each name had character, with its strong regional tang. There seemed a clot in his stomach, like a lump of blood, at the thought of returning home. When he had arrived in Bombay he had felt that home had been lost forever. Now even though he was returning, he still thought it inaccessible; it had now withered into the destination of clandestine visits that had been arranged with endless petty lies, a place of abortions. Just for three or four days; he knew that the ecstasy of arrival would not compensate for the emptiness of departure.

Atri looked out at the ugliness, the absolute desolation of the city. Ten-storeyed grey box flats with slime climbing up the pipes that took the shit away, box verandahs of bored, lonely women and men blankly surveying the deformed world while waiting all day for TV to start. He looked across at Sheela, at her oddly magnetic face, now a little unsure. 'Come and sit here.' She did. They were alone in their compartment. 'How should we begin in Delhi?'

'I don't know.'

'First, by getting into bed.'

She tried to smile. 'I've no idea what's going to happen.'

Atri could say nothing. He put his arm around her. In Lucknow, at their last parting, she had cried much, silently. He had been surprised and guilty. 'We'll hunt around, tomorrow itself.'

'Bombay was so nice.'

'You mustn't worry. This abortion thing will get over really fast.'

Sheela looked up into Atri's face. 'Yesterday I caught a local train for Bandra to meet an old friend, Anjali, have you ever met her, she's pretty boring. In the train, just above the last row of seats, there was a small board, an ad for a clinic, it said abortions for only seventy.'

'But we couldn't've gone to some unknown dirty place.' There would've been grime and guilt perhaps, in a small, harshly-lit waiting room, the lovelessness in the faces of other almost-fathers by error, and a dusty telephone that didn't work. Outside the world would have continued to move like the sea at Bombay, an unending, purposeless ebb and flow, totally heedless of the anguish of men. 'There are also some Marie Stopes Clinics.'

'Who was Marie Stopes?'

'I don't know, some do-gooder.'

Their conversation was staccato throughout the journey. The expressions of tenderness and concern were awkward, almost false. The silences seemed eternal, the depression insidious. When they caught themselves looking at each other, their mouths would contort, as though bitter with remembrances. The hours moved, the landscape changed, and the skies, Surat, Baroda, Ratlam, Kota, fleeting, fugitive visions of the hinterland, and for Atri the cloud heaved a little only when he saw the polluted morning sky in the near distance over Delhi.

They went to the hostel first. Even Sheela looked gladder in the familiar surroundings. 'Ugly as ever,' she said happily.

'I'll look in at about five.' Atri went home. His parents were surprised and pleased. 'Some Marathi hero was born or died or something. Just a few days off. I couldn't get through on the phone from Bombay, horrible lines, so I just turned up.' Almost immediately he telephoned Anand at his office. His mother grumbled, 'Not even half an hour at home and you want to meet your friends. Especially that Anand.'

'I'll be back for lunch, Ma.'

'I'm honoured.'

Atri took the car keys from the table in his father's room. He felt happy to be driving again on Delhi's wide roads. Delhi was not particularly lovable, but it was familiar. And for him happiness had always been fragile and unexpected, even unsettling, like a time bomb. Birth, education, a job, marriage, the petty adjustments of marriage, a home of one's own, the breeding of children—he found the conventions of this circle meaningless, and the obtuseness of the world that arranged this insane succession galled him. He had grown up in one spot, had grown accustomed to it, like a finger to stroking a scar, and then had been wrenched away to an alien place. Rootlessness was agonizing enough within, yet the conventions of existence externalized it, and buttressed the agony with objective symbols for the eye.

Anand was an architect. His office was the size of the lavatory of a shabby restaurant. Five young architects sat in that small room. Their tables were six-inch ledges of some black synthetic thing. Everything was built in or recessed, 'maximum use of space'. Each architect earned vast sums.

'Let's go out for coffee somewhere.' The cafe they chose smelt of chhole and sour milk. Grease and forearms had dulled the scarlet decolam of the table.

'So you couldn't bear your training or what?'

'Your telegram read "Ma in uppal with fart attack". I hope that was unintentional.'

Anand laughed. 'It was a phonogram. Be happy it reached.'

'Sheela's pregnant, she thinks.' Anand's smile disappeared. 'We didn't know where to go in Bombay. You once said you knew some decent places.'

'That's bad.' Anand looked away for a while, out to the hive of offices across the dry fountain. 'You don't want to marry now?'

'No.'

'I know one good place. Costs about fifteen hundred, all told, air-conditioned and so on. You want to go tomorrow? I'll ring her up from office, for, what, eleven tomorrow morning?'

'What's her name?'

'Dr Singh. I call her Aarti. She's quite sexy. Has degrees from some funny-sounding place in Europe.'

'Anyone you know has been to her?'

'Ha ha.'

'Fifteen hundred is quite a lot.'

'You must pay for your sins.'

The flashy waiter brought coffee. Anand said, 'I feel sorry for Sheela, though I never really liked her. She must be having a bad time, tension etcetera.'

'Yet when you first met her,' Atri smiled, 'you'd hoped I wasn't serious about her. You'd said, remember that late-late-night coffee at the Emperor Oak, that "she's just not in our class, boy. It would be like marrying a servant, you know, someone one loses one's virginity to".'

'Yes, and you'd said, "male or female servant?"' They laughed. They were conscious of the baseness of their remarks, but also that there was no one else to hear them. Anand continued, 'She'd do very well for Micky.'

'Because you dislike him too.' They laughed again. Anand was an old friend.

Atri continued, 'Micky's very violent and...aggressive...in... expressions of love. In Lucknow sometimes he'd dash to some bush just to pluck a flower for her. An exhibitionist.' Which Sheela had seemed to like, he thought.

Anand lit a cigarette. 'Sheela's very young. And for most Indian girls, sex is not casual. Did you mislead her perhaps?' he looked away at the man behind the coffee percolator. 'Perhaps she assumed, or expected, marriage.'

'I don't know. We were always flippant.' Except that time

in Lucknow, when she had wept. Most of the time Sheela had been so happy and somehow appealing, that Atri had sometimes wanted to cause pain, subtle and complex, to bewilder her so that she could reach, for a while, his emptiness.

Anand exhaled luxuriously. 'But good you aren't marrying. Take away that body, and she's quite thick.'

Anand is saying what Ma said, thought Atri, what an epitaph for Sheela, now she seemed to belong to the dead. He lit a cigarette, though he rarely smoked.

10.50 next morning. The opulence of the clinic was intimidating. It was in one of South Delhi's new mansions, vast and vulgar. Unsure of themselves, Sheela and Atri walked from the car close together, subtly touching each other in what would once have been erotic, back of hand against outside of thigh, breast against triceps. A large, unweeded garden, a carved wooden door with a one-foot Khajuraho woman for a handle, the chill of effective air-conditioning, a cold, hard woman at a white desk, Atri inhaled deeply to down the bobbing nervousness.

'We have an appointment with Dr Singh.'

The woman pushed her huge spectacles up and consulted two diaries. Sheela vanished through another door. Atri mumbled 'Good luck,' but she didn't acknowledge him in any way, perhaps she hadn't heard. She was in her bright yellow salwar-kameez. Leafing through glossies on the coffee table Atri waited and wondered. Couldn't they tell from the urine these days that a girl was pregnant? He and Sheela were so ignorant. Then his mind wandered, pregnant women actually piddled out babies the size of cells, and pregnancy could be checked by examining piss under a microscope for these babies, who, wallowing happily in maternal urine but stifled under glass, waved at the monstrously distorted human eye above them. With each pregnancy actually a million babies were born but they all died when their heads exploded against the porcelain of the commode. The one who survived hung on to the moist walls of the womb with its claws.

Sheela emerged, expressionless. Atri stood up, but she didn't look at anybody. She said something to the cold, hard woman, then they moved out, stopped outside at the Khajuraho handle. 'Well, what happened?' But he wasn't really interested. He wanted to say, maybe Dr Singh cooed to you and skilfully slipped in two fingers and pulled out a foetus with Micky's mind and Satish's face.

'We'll have to come back tomorrow to meet Dr Singh, she's only in in the mornings, but the report itself'll be ready by about four this evening.' That seemed to leave Atri in limbo. 'Perhaps we should go and have coffee somewhere,' he suggested, 'and get into bed or something, I don't know.' Sheela said nothing. While driving he looked at her often. Cocooned in himself, he had never considered her loneliness or her wishes. 'You like babies a lot, no? All that cooing and nephew's piddle. You'd've liked this child?' Sheela continued to look away. 'But marriage wouldn't've been possible, we'd've ended up like my parents.' He stopped, out of a kind of boredom.

After a while Sheela said, 'Do they, do your parents know about all this?'

'No, of course not.'

'I want to tell them. That you made me pregnant and that you want me to abort.'

'Okay, sure. And remember to tell yours too.' Atri parked badly under the derisive eye of the car park attendant. The cafe seemed to be full of schoolgirls. 'Your telling them will hurt them, that's all, perhaps confuse them a little.'

'So?' Sheela lit a cigarette.

'Remember how I taught you to inhale?' She exhaled into his face. He felt faintly aroused, and continued, 'Didn't someone say that abortion was the fruit of lust. If we had been in love, then we'd've had the baby. And if we hadn't lusted then we wouldn't have slept together.' She closed her eyes and leaned back, her hair disturbing the leaves of some potted shrub behind her. She stretched out her legs and continued to exhale in the direction of his face. Her cold face could've been tired, or disinterested; or a mask hiding her cold, controlled dislike. Atri again saw her perfectly, like he had once at Lucknow station, the brown throat, the firm, almost hard, upper arms. Ideally he wanted a sort of djinn or familiar, who would appear when required, in the guise that Atri desired, glut each of his sexual caprices, and then leave him absolutely alone; he would never impose himself on Atri; when not needed, he wouldn't even exist. Wanting to hurt and be hurt, Atri picked up Sheela's leg by her calf, pushed off her sandal, pinched her skin hard through her salwar. He rested her foot on his chair, pressed his crotch tense against her heel, his knees stubborn against her leg, and bent down and kissed, and bit, her unclean toes. Only such an act could silence the schoolgirls at the next table. Eyes still closed, but Sheela was smiling.

Of course they left instantly. They were laughing excitedly on the way to the car. Atri stopped for bananas. 'Here, have some phallic symbols.' They giggled and gobbled two each. This was an amazing way to end, thought Atri, of course it was ending, no more threats to those dreams of dispossession. In the car he licked the salt off Sheela's neck and felt her warm stomach beneath the kameez. 'Shall we name the foetus before they kill it? Let's call it Hawas, you know, Lust.'

Sheela said, 'If I'd kept my thighs crossed, I'd've had you begging for marriage from day one.'

'Why, I'll still beg in front of you, not for anything, just whimper and beg.'

'Then beg in front of me while I tell your parents about the mess we're in.' But this kind of conversation always embarrassed Sheela.

'Why don't we go to Anand's flat? Now we don't even need condoms.' Atri got out of the car to look for a phone. One chemist lied and said that his phone wasn't working, one huge general store simply refused. Atri succeeded at a bookshop run by a mother and her daughter. 'Anand, speaking from Connaught.

Went there this morning. They'll give us the report at four or so. I say, is the key to your flat still under that brass thing?'

'You'll never learn.'

'Now we don't even need condoms.'

'My sister's been staying with me for weeks. She left her Hyderabad job and is now looking for another.'

'God, she can have mine anytime.'

'She might be out, in which case she'll have taken the key.'

'Any other place you can think of?'

'Your ugly Ambassador, you monkey.'

'Tch, bye now. I'll ring up again.'

'Good luck.'

When he returned to Sheela, she had changed. Again a wan, dying face, eyes crinkling with cigarette smoke. 'You're not on heat any more?'

'I want to go back to the hostel.'

'Okay.' Atri moved the car out. Even the demands of lust are enervating, he thought; he would make no claims beyond them. 'When shall we go for the report? Tomorrow morning?'

'Okay.'

Atri returned home. 'See, I told you I'd be back for lunch,' he told his mother. At lunch his father asked, 'How's the job?'

'Dull and meaningless, but I expected nothing else.'

'It's important to like your job. If you really don't like this you should think again about your PhD.'

'Yes, let's see.' After lunch Atri and his father played two games of chess. Then Atri wandered from room to room, opening cupboards and unlocking memories; a bewildering afternoon in which he often thought that his past had been happy, and then wondered whether he thought so just because the past was irretrievable. In the evening he watched TV with his parents. He looked at them steadily gazing at the TV without registering any of its belches, and wondered about their youth. Perhaps they had been like him, perhaps he would finish up like them, in front of a TV, and at the point of his surrender to that uncaring sea, its hush would become a roar.

At the clinic the next morning the report said that Sheela was not pregnant. Dr Singh turned out to be fortyish, aggressive and revolting. 'Definitely not a pregnancy. Your period could be delayed for a variety of reasons. Mental tension or some illness. Get yourself thoroughly checked up. No, payment outside, please.'

Outside the clinic they paused uncertainly beneath a jacaranda in bloom. 'So are you ill, or what're you tense about?' Atri smiled.

Sheela bit her lip. 'It's really odd. I suppose this test was foolproof. Maybe I should really get that check-up.' In the car she said, 'I feel weird. All that tension for nothing.'

'Coffee somewhere I think. But not yesterday's cafe, perhaps.'

Sheela laughed. 'No, let's go there.' They moved off. Atri was content to let things be. She repeated, half to herself, 'It's strange.' They chose the same table. He asked, 'Do you want to go to Bombay again?' She looked away. 'No, that would be very funny. I just want to sort of stay here and relax.' They had very little to say to each other, there seemed no cause for celebration. After coffee they had nowhere to go so he dropped her back at the hostel. 'I'll probably go back tomorrow, I'll write from Bombay.'

'Stay a day or two more,' Sheela asked unconvincingly.

'No, we'd better leave each other alone for while, to recover from this one.' She laughed, waved and went lightly up the stairs.

On the train to Bombay, returning to the unknown city and an empty future, Atri was almost nauseous with depression. He curled in his berth and was assaulted by savage, masochistic images of, among others, Mrs Karve. He wanted to be beaten senseless, to be deprived of his mind so that he didn't have to think.

Eight empty days in Bombay, the city of dead rats and smegma; on a few evenings rummy with Mrs Karve, on a few others watching the patch of Australia on the wall from his bed and absorbing the grunts and clinks from the Youth Club next door. Then, for their next phase of training, Atri and Mrs Karve moved to Madras. Madras was humid and alien-tongued. The new Training Institute there was on the edge of the city, close to the beach, girdled by fishermen. A small, clean, featureless room, 'maximum use of space', the same classes, in the evenings slow walks in the compound, watching disinterested gardeners trying to create a lawn out of rubble. Atri contracted dengue. The fever ravaged him for seven days. While Mrs Karve attended class, he lay alone watching the sanatorium-white ceiling, juggling with bittersweet images of his past. In the evenings Mrs Karve brought company and chatter, because she had nowhere to go. The fever procured an insidious intimacy between them. They listened to the delightful hyperbole of Urdu ghazals on her recorder and watched the evening pass the window. The songs spoke of loss and despair, the best of them creating a fleeting grace out of these ashes. *When I first saw you / the world moved on but I halted / and I haven't moved on since then, / waiting, still waiting / for you to move with me.* At moments, the music and Mrs Karve combined to stir him gently, like the memory, or the shadow, of another desire.

At the end of that week, they had some days off. Mr Karve emerged out of the hinterland, dull and good looking. Mrs Karve disappeared with him. One Sunday at twilight they took Atri to the beach in a noisy, smelling taxi. Madras, his parents had married here, he remembered. He sat timid and bent on a bench, like an invalid, knees together. The sea breeze revived his feverishness, the late-evening sky was a mess of black and gold. Behind him the Karves joined the babble of children around the kulfiwala. Here the sea was louder than at Bombay; it did not whisper, but roared its unconcern. In his tiredness, Atri half-smiled and prayed for the decline of all desire.

seven

~

# THE DEEPEST BLUE

## K. R. MEERA

*Translated from the Malayalam by J. Devika*

The experience of love that I'm going to describe is the strangest you'll have ever encountered. So here's advance warning: chaste wives (in the satisavitri mould) and strictly monogamous men (in the maryaadaapurushottam mould) are advised against reading this account. I will not be responsible for whatever breaches of morality that may result from reading it. This thing called 'chastity' is so desecrated these days. The days of flawless devotion to husbands are over. What wives do these days, through email, the cell phone, and the landline, when their husbands aren't around the house! The Sreeramachandras, the ones who know no doe-eyed damsel other than their wives, and the Jewels of Feminine Virtue, alas, have all disappeared, root, branch and all, from the face of this earth. I, too, am quite saddened by all this. I'm sincerely fired by the desire to write stories that salute the few well-born, homely women of virtue (so rare are they—so scarce) who walk with assured gait and firm step upon the tightrope of morality, even as this world is going all topsy-turvy. But then, fiction isn't life, ah, a fact that renders one so powerless! A life—that's easier to end as we please. Not even a mangy dog would be curious about its denouement. But when it comes to a story, the game is entirely different. The story's movement upon paper is like a serpent's movement upon a rock. An unpredictable slithering. If it goes wrong, that's it. Readers will pull out daggers. And every other wayfaring Marykutty will step in, to perform a critique. So then, why bother with all the nonsense? For that reason, there's no story on offer. In its place, a bit of life, a burning sliver of experience.

This is experience, and must therefore be honestly recounted. Wherever honesty thrives, morality must decline. So, before proceeding any further—caution! There's still time. You can stop reading right now. It's the readers' responsibility to hold tight to their chastity and peace of mind so that these don't fall in a heap on the floor. Reading ahead may adversely affect children, pregnant women, heart patients, and my husband: they are advised against venturing any further.

Only the firm-hearted are advised to proceed.

~

I've already told you. A sliver of experience—of love. That too, a burning speck. I loved him. The name will remain a secret. If it doesn't remain a secret, my husband will leave me. My children will grow up suffering their stepmother's taunts. Friends and relatives will hate me. My husband may even finish me off with poison. I'm not worried about all this. Death doesn't look like a problem to me. If this life ends, the next one will begin. That's all there is to it. But no, not when I remember him. A terrible weakness overpowers me then. He, poor soul, someone who's suffered much pain in this birth, and perhaps in former births too. Someone upon whom life weighed so heavily that he became a hermit. Should I drag such a man into all this? Should I throw him to the sharks? No. Therefore, be so kind as to forgive me for not identifying him. After all, what's in a name?

Let me tell you of our love. Make no mistake; this is not my first love. I have been in love perpetually. Before marriage and after. My love is a languid serpent, an utterly venomous one. For a long time it lay still, coiled upon its own body, biding its time, lying in wait. For someone. Who, one didn't know. Someone. Who wouldn't die of my fangs. Who was deep blue by birth. The three-eyed one. Never saw him. Ever. Those whom I met were all false Vasudevas. Ones whose bluish tinge vanished under a tight kiss. Each time it was a mistake I made. I moulted; I left each one of them behind. To those who tried to hold fast, I gave my decaying, old, scaly skin. No one saw me, no one really touched me. They measured the length and breadth of the skin, heaved huge sighs of relief—what a huge poisonous snake, how lucky that it slid away—and were consoled. The silver spots upon my sloughed-off skins glistened in the daylight as they lay in the backyards of their lives.

Let that be. I will speak about us. We met late. He'd become a hermit by then. And I, married, and a mother of two. People who had gone a long way down opposite paths. We'd have to walk back, start all over again together. If that's possible, that is. But that isn't possible. If that was, human beings would have tried. What distance would they not walk back, if it was possible?

I will speak of how we found each other. The partitioning of the family property brought me some money. I insisted to my husband that we buy an old naalukettu house. One like the house I was born and raised in. A house with doors so low that one could enter only with head bowed, with a ceiling so low that it could be touched by merely raising your arm. My house was like that—a cool, breezy house. The wind from the river used to rush in through the south window and whirl about, flustered at not finding a way out. That house doesn't exist any more. It was wiped out by lightning. As the flames leapt up from one side, my mother, sisters and I, picked up all that we could and ran out. That was the month of the November rains. It was raining so hard, a drop would have filled a pot. But the house didn't stop burning. It fought against the downpour and went down blazing, reduced to ashes. My father burned to death inside. The place where it stood became a void. In my father's place was another void, a greater one.

I wanted a house like that one. We advertised in the newspapers many times. Several sellers wrote back to us. We would go to see each house on offer.

'Why not buy this one?'

Each time, my husband would be enthused.

'No...' I replied, each time. 'This isn't what I have in my mind...'

'That's going to be only in your mind.' His tone turned accusing after a while. 'It's only a fantasy.'

That house is real; it stands somewhere. Of that I am sure. The same house that I have in my mind. The one with the serpent grove on its south side and the kili tree on its east, upon which lush tangles of wild jasmine thrive. Where the sleepy murmur of birds and the hot sighs of the snakes enter, if the southside window is opened at night. Funny, but I also knew that he'd be there. Yes, I knew all that well before. All of it. He's the one who didn't know. Poor man. He lived in the lightness of his ignorance, detached. All alone, in that naalukettu house, with its many windows. I sought him out there, asked him to name a price for the house, but he didn't recognize me.

We had gone to those parts to look at another house. I didn't like it. So on the way back, the broker suggested, 'There's another house nearby... It's something that might appeal to you, madam...but the owner is a sannyasi...what a pity, he won't sell.'

'Let's go over,' I insisted, 'maybe he will sell?'

My husband decided to try. He turned into the road the broker had pointed out to us. The car stopped in front of the tile-roofed gateway. A thrill ran through my pores at the very first sight of the house. This was it, I knew. The tile-roofed gateway built of sandstone blocks. The curving doorway. The rough, gravelly village road. Paddy fields opening out on the other side. The water channel running by the road in which tiny fish swam.

From the fields rose a clay-scented breeze. There must be a path north of the yard, I mused, and that must lead to the river. A kaitha bush growing in the river, one that tumbled onto the riverbank in riotous abandon. There must be waterfowls that tiptoed out when no one was around. The kaitha must be in full bloom now. I could catch a whiff of its scent, though the kaitha hadn't bloomed yet. My nerves tingled.

We entered the gateway. The garden was full of trees and cool languor. Dusk was falling. A greenish dark hovered about. Birds cooed, hurrying to roost. In the dim light, I saw him sitting on a floor mat in the distant veranda. There was a harmonium before him, and ten little children gathered around him. It was a music class. He turned towards us, his left hand still on the harmonium. My husband and the broker went up to the veranda to speak with him. I didn't. I stood inside the gateway, near the kili tree upon which the wild jasmine grew. The jasmine burst into bloom, as if from a sudden thrill. A forest-caller flew up suddenly, calling out loud and long, flashing its bright tail feathers.

He stood up. He was clad in an ochre dhoti; an ochre towel covered his shoulders. His beard reached his chest; a long mane of hair fell to his shoulders. I didn't look at his face. The blood in my body raced through its tiny rivulets. I stepped out of the gateway hurriedly. I got into the car, panting. Nearly weeping. A terrible bitterness welled up within me.

My husband and the broker returned.

'He is not selling. He's giving it away to some ashram...'

I made no answer. My husband had liked him, he said so. He's a scholar, a gentleman, well-off. But an ascetic. How radiant his face! What deep calm in his voice! No ordinary ascetic, this.

'Let's go,' I said, sickened. 'I have a headache.'

My husband started the car. I closed my eyes tight. The pain was real. But it wasn't in my head. It throbbed in my chest and loins. Piercing pain. Not pain, really. Piercing, stabbing desire. Desire smouldering, like specks of flame eating slowly, slowly, into raw flesh. I want to bear a child in my womb. I want to give birth. To a son. His son. I meditated. His face. His form. What would he look like? How would he be? The hermit's sperm; the slut's ovum. Renunciation and desire, in equal measure.

You've got it, I suppose? I'm terribly decadent.

~

The unmarried have keener eyesight. Once you're married, it diminishes. When he was my lover, my husband wrote four or five whole essays about a small birthmark I have on the little finger of my right hand. That trivial birthmark was indeed exalted! Subject to much unnecessary coddling, it turned into a Movement. But the moment the thali—the marriage pendant—was tied around my neck like a noose, it reverted to being a humble birthmark. He never saw it again.

I've already told you. Marriage weakens the eyesight. He forgot the birthmark, the flowery words he'd uttered about it, and our romance itself. Marriage weakens the memory, too.

It's thirteen years now since we got married. You can imagine the state of his eyesight. He's shortsighted. Never notices my face or its expressions. I was uneasy, like a snake stifled in a wicker basket. The music of the makuti came to me, loud and clear. I had to escape. I need to slither out to the place from where the sound rose. But how? I squirmed, uneasy within the four walls of the house. I scolded both my daughters; accused them of lacking discipline; reminded them that chastity was their greatest wealth.

Then I shut myself in my bedroom and tossed about in bed.

I wanted to see him. But how? There was a day's gap between us. The distance of a long journey. He's not selling the house. It was being given away to some ashram. What excuse could I possibly fashion to go over? Clouds of smoke smothered my brain.

'What are you thinking about?' my husband asked.

'That was a lovely house.'

'Oh, so you haven't forgotten it?'

I shut my eyes tightly. No. Not yet. How could I? Exuberant wild jasmine springs into sight whenever I shut my eyes. I see the veranda. A luxuriant crown of tangled hair.

'The ascetic won't sell it. And even if he does, let's not buy it. He's the last heir; no child has been born in that house since him...'

My eyes opened. My womb throbbed.

'Let's go there once more, let's try again...'

'Don't I have anything better to do?' He was angry. I slid closer to him on the bed and wrapped my arms around him.

'Please...'

'You are too much. Enough!'

'If he isn't selling, let it be. Let's just go and see the house... We could build one like it...'

He agreed. I knew he would. There was no other way. Because this is not fiction. This is life. What one writes after experience—that's fiction. Experiencing what's written—that's life. That's the inconvenience of life. And the freedom of fiction.

~

Let that be. He came with me. We went there again. The same house. The tile-roofed gateway, the kili tree, the wild jasmine. A hundred flowers with no one to pluck them. Another world inside the gateway. The retreating sunlight outside. The languid dusk inside. Outside, the clamour of folk returning from the market. Inside, the silence of roosting birds.

He walked ahead. I followed him, slowly. In the courtyard, a sacred basil stood, as tall as a man. On the half-wall, delicate white mandaaram flowers, plucked. The parijatham bloomed in the front yard. Their fragrance borne upon the breeze. My heart beat hard. My stomach ached as if from terrible hunger.

My husband pressed a finger to the doorbell. He came to the door. A huge man. Ochre dhoti, ochre towel, sacred ash smeared on the forehead and chest. The long hair, the long beard, silver starting to streak it.

'You?'

He smiled. My husband folded his hands, saluting.

'Come...do have a seat...'

'You remember me, I hope?' my husband asked.

'Yes...'

I gazed intently at him. Nothing new to the eye. This wooden house. Him. The luminous smile. The meditative eyes. The shoulder covered with fine hair, under the ochre towel. The stooping posture—he was very tall. All this, I've long known.

'You aren't selling the house, isn't that so?' my husband said with a smile.

'My wife liked it a lot. Could we look around?'

'Why not? Do come in.'

He led the way inside. 'Most of it is shut up. It's swept only once or twice a month, so there'll be a lot of dust.'

My husband tripped on one of the wooden steps.

'Be careful,' he said, 'the house is really old. Don't hit your head.'

I ignored the comment haughtily. Don't you teach me. I know. After the sitting room comes the central room. Step into the veranda of the central room, and you reach the central courtyard. The platform in the middle on which the sacred basil grew. In the rain, the tinkling of rainwater upon the bronze metal-leaf on the roof-edge. I know. I've known.

My husband asked him something about the carvings on

the wooden door. He turned to respond. I walked ahead, not needing a guide. The northern door beyond the kitchen and the central room where the mortar and pestle are kept. I placed a hand on the bolt. He suddenly inclined his head, looking at me.

'That won't open, it can't be opened.'

He walked up to me.

'I want to see the river,' I said.

He looked at me more closely. For a second. I too saw in his eyes a female form clad in a shimmering sari of green silk, her hair coiled behind. That was it. He looked away.

'Go around through the front door...that's easier,' he said. I felt annoyed suddenly, as if he had shrunk me! He wasn't even trying to open the door. I put my hand on the door and tried to loosen the bolt, hitting the wooden planks with my elbow.

'Don't open it. It can't be closed again if you do.' He tried to stop me.

But before he had even finished speaking, how wonderful, the bolt loosened. The door opened. He looked a bit startled. And then, his detached air reappeared, and he smiled.

'Oh...so it opened?'

'It did...' I stood there, triumphant.

'It's been years. The bottom must have rotted...'

I did not reply; I stepped out into the yard. Darkness amidst the dense foliage of kilichundan mango trees. Beyond that, another tree, the poovarasu; and further on, a bramble fence, then the river. The kaitha bushes stood at the edge of the property. They were in bloom. The river breeze wafted by, delicate and fragrant as a flower. I became free as if all my bonds had been loosened. Where is the serpent grove? Where is the njaaval tree?

I reached the sacred grove, a verdant umbrella open to the sky. Mildly swaying vines glided down from the naagadanti. I wanted to creep under its branches. How cool it was! The wet leaves. The moist soil. How would it feel to lie on the ground, on the bare ground? The grasshoppers would leap up from the greenery below. Onto my head first. Then onto my forehead. And then onto my breasts. A little snake might hatch from its egg, pressing upon the warmth of my belly. A dark-skinned one. I tried to imagine its face. Its forked tongue flicking in a relaxed manner from its mouth. Pretty little milk teeth. The next thing I knew I was bitten by a snake. You won't believe it when I tell you. I can't believe it either. That's the difference between fiction and life. Life, that's fiction written at some unknown time. I was bitten on the left leg, exactly where I used to wear an anklet as a child. I think it was a cobra. I didn't see. Two little teeth had sunk in. That's all that happened. I stood where I was. I broke into a heavy sweat, as if I'd run a long way. The spot where I had been bitten felt as though an oilwick had been lit on it. I was in flames even as the sweat streamed down my body.

Quite like how my house had blazed in the rain.

~

Later, I realized. Every love affair needs a go-between. The beloved's medium, that which reveals her heart to her lover. The snake was revealing my message.

I was lying on his veranda when I came to. When I opened my eyes his face was close to mine. The depth of his eyes, the proud outline of his nose. The ascetic detachment. The sage-like calm. He was tying a tourniquet above the bite mark. He lowered his face on to the wound, sucked out the poison and spat it out. I was in pain and I rejoiced in it. I saw everything as if through a prism. The ascetic's face at my feet. My blood on his lips. A strange sight. Strange indeed. I told you, love is like that. Strange, from top to toe. Astonishingly so.

'Geeta... Geeta...' my husband was calling out to me, worried.

'She's opened her eyes...now there's nothing to be concerned about,' he said.

'The venom hasn't moved up her body. That was fortunate... take her to the doctor quickly...'

He gave the keys of the north gate to my husband so he could bring the car into the front yard. My husband went off. I came awake from my stupor. I lay there, watching him wash my blood from his mouth, pour water on his face, sprinkle it on his head, as if to purify himself. A cool breeze wafted in, redolent with the fragrance of wild jasmine and gandharajan. His eyes were on the garden path. I looked at him intently. He was magnetic. His face was radiant. What did he feel when he pressed his lips on my wound? What sensation did my blood evoke on his tongue? I ached badly, from head to toe. My heart screamed. I groaned. He turned and looked at me. With compassionate eyes.

'Yes, what is it?'

I moved my lips.

'Water?'

I stretched out my arm.

He picked up the water jar and came up to where I lay on the floor. He sat down next to me, knees folded as if in a funeral rite. Light lay scattered within those eyes. Eyes rapt in contemplation. Eyes that did not look at me. I warned you early on. I'm shameless. The mother of two girls. The wife of a forty-year-old man. Impossibly bold. Immeasurably assertive. I was in a hurry. My husband could return any minute. My arms curved around his neck. My teeth sunk into his lips as I pulled his face down towards me. Two of my best venom teeth. Believe it or not, he turned completely blue.

∽

The many lives I have traversed, shedding many outer skins. I crawl on. From one to another. Over prickly cacti, rough boulders. Above mountains and trees. Over wet, fallen leaves, wilted flowers. One life at a time. He is present in each one of them. Always of the same colour. The deepest blue.

While convalescing after being bitten by the snake, these things passed through my mind. I was amused by them. Two beings wandering through space and time searching for the other. Who finally met, but did not recognize each other. The secrets of life are strange. I thought of him whenever my husband and children appeared before me. His eyes. His eyes, deep enough for me to dip into and rise again.

'Why did you have to go there at that time, my dear?' my husband asked. Whenever he was free, he would sit beside me, stroking my forehead. I held fast to his hands.

'Did I bother you?'

'It's not that...it hurts to see you like this, so weak...'

'Anyway let's not think of buying a house again... Let's give it up. If we put the money in the bank, there'll be peace of mind at least...'

I didn't reply. Why did I need a house any more? I didn't seek the house, I sought the owner. Selling or buying a house wasn't an issue any more! There was just one issue: him. The distance between us. The distance of years, ages. How was I going to get him back? Each time I shut my eyes, his face appeared—the face in which the bluish tinge keeps spreading, slowly, slowly. Right before me, close enough to touch. I stretched out my hands and touched him again and again. True. And strange.

I looked closely at myself in the mirror. What did I see? A female form. A woman who has lived some three decades and a half. My mother bore me in her womb, gave birth to me, nursed me at her breast. I crawled on my knees; sat up; stood up; walked; ate; slept; grew; reproduced. And now I draw close to old age and death.

My form made me laugh. Who is this? A woman, with her hair tied up or down; clad in a sari or a mundu; lining her eyes with kohl, and touching herself up with face powder. A woman who sautéed cabbage thoran for lunch; who sprayed perfume on her husband's handkerchiefs and folded them neatly; who combed out the lice from the girls' hair, braiding them nicely; who never failed to give her husband his daily dose of high blood pressure drugs on time. What is this woman? Why was she born? Why is she living? This forty-year-old man with his slightly greying hair and these girls aged ten and twelve, who are they to her? She herself, who is she, really?

Who am I? What am I? These questions vexed me. So, the first opportunity I got, I went to see him again, without my husband's knowledge. I went there alone. As usual, it was evening when I reached the house. The languorous dusk. The sky stretched above, bluish, as if consumed by venom.

He was preparing for evening worship. I entered through the open front door without waiting for permission.

He started, seeing me. The memory of the bite still stung. Inside was a large image of Goddess Tripurasundari, almost as tall as a human being. The goddess sat astride a roaring lion, bedecked with jewels. A garland of white mandaaram flowers hung around her neck. The ceremonial dish was full of camphor cubes. The lamps were filled with oil and decked with oil wicks.

He got up slowly. He looked extraordinarily imposing. Extraordinarily powerful. Someone beyond the reach of simple touch.

'Come...' he said.

He walked over to a sofa in the sitting room and sat down. His fingers strummed the veena kept on the teapoy next to the sofa. It emitted an awesome sound. I was amused. This is someone who would not be defeated.

'Take a seat... Did you come alone?'

'Yes...'

I sat down on the sofa opposite him. I kept looking at him. He never looked at me. The seconds flew between us.

'This house is not for sale...' he said quickly.

I laughed. He suddenly looked straight into my eyes, unwaveringly.

'Do you think you are rich enough to quote a price for this house?'

I laughed out aloud.

'Tell me the truth, what is on your mind? Why have you come here again?'

What a thing to ask. Why have I come, indeed? I felt dispirited. Well, is there a man in this world who doesn't disappoint? Ask how I came to be here, I whispered in my mind. It took a lot of trouble. A lot of lies. Many obstacles had to be overcome. Many concessions had to be given; many compromises had to be made. Just think of it. That moment. That house. That desolation. That dusk. The two of us. Two beings who had grown weary in their search for each other, across many lives. The moment in which we came face to face. Intense, ardent, volatile. But what happened, really? He did not remember a thing. Did not recognize anything. I alone knew. He ought to have been the one to know. He should have come in search of me. He should have removed my outer skins; he should have received my venom in his palms. But what did he do? He ran away to Tripurasundari. He worshipped her, adored her. Devoted his whole life to her. And me? I sought him through many lives. Like a serpent which had lost the gem it guarded, I lurched and staggered. Well, is there a woman in this world who has been loved fairly?

I tried to say something. I don't remember the words. Surely, they were about love. And about this life. He spoke about asceticism. He warned me about the soul, about sacred vows. I challenged him, ridiculed him, asking, where does asceticism lie, in the body or the soul? I don't know what he made of that. He may or may not have understood. I kissed him forcibly. It had been easier to open the old wooden door! But even that opened in the end. I challenged him again to rise above the body. He accepted it and kissed me. To speak of his kiss, well—it wasn't spectacular. I forgave him for that. Men should kiss with their souls, not with their lips. I had taught him that, in each of our lives. Poor thing, he forgot all of it. I must remind him again. I will make the ascetic separate himself from his body. I'll make him an unadorned soul. I broke into laughter as I held him. No change at all. Aeons have passed, life after life has withered and drooped, but nothing has changed. His hands, his neck, his chest. It's the same as before.

I've already told you. This love story is a strange one. I sought him madly. And finally I found him. But he didn't remember me. How was I to remind him? I had no ring to stir the memory, no jewel, no gift retained from our past that could remind him. I had only my desire for him; my ancient memory of him. Would that be enough to rouse the ascetic from his trance? And that too, this man. This powerful, undefeated man. He who reduced the God of Love to a pile of ashes. It is not easy to lead a man into physical love. Especially this one, who was Tripurasundari's slave. But, I've told you, he is my other half; he has only half my strength. I led him as far as the bedroom; as far as nakedness.

'Thirty years...thirty years since the vows...' he panted. That was just before our bodies were to join. The very moment he'd gone beyond his body. The moment in which I awaited his embrace, upon the wooden cot. A moment in which but a finger's distance separated us. One single moment.

He woke up, suddenly.

'No...' he said, decisively. 'I can't do it...the Devi's image in my mind...'

He dressed without looking at me and went out. That moment. Just think. The dusk before the November rain fell. The sky smitten by venom. A cage with wooden walls. A woman lies waiting, all her outer skins discarded. For him. For his touch, his tenderness. His surrender. I lay there, sapped, like a snake with a broken spine. The darkness built its lair around me. A fruitless life.

The wind blew hard. The leaves of the money-vine clinging to the mango tree fluttered feebly in the garden.

The rain must have come and gone; the fireflies must have flitted about; the midnight bird must have trilled aloud. I did not know.

At dawn, I dressed and returned to my husband and children.

~

I've told you. This love is not only strange, but also painful. Anyway, what is love without pain? It must ache as if your bosom has been cleaved apart. The gnawing pain from jealousy's sharp-toothed saw. The scorching pain of the embers of loss. I will tear out my wings and fly to him. The blood will flow from my torn wings. His white mandaaram blossoms will turn red from my blood. I will defeat him with blood and pain.

I was jealous of Tripurasundari. She stole my man. He's mesmerized by her image. He calls her by her thousand names, yet his mind is not full. She is but a feeling. Nothing but his imagination. When I remembered that, I burned. Frustration fuelled my rage; my rage fuelled my revenge. My feet ached when I walked; my fingers ached when I ate my food. Every pore of my body ached. He is mine. His soft fingers, his immaculate feet, his radiant eyes. I own all of this, I alone. I have no knowledge of black magic. If I had, I would have turned him into a bird and locked him in a cage. I would have made him into a nail, hammered deep into my forehead. I would have turned him into an embryo and carried him in my womb. I would not have left him to worship any Tripurasundari; I would have distilled him into a terrible poison and died drinking it.

I wrote to him:

> I dream of your death. One night I will arrive at your house with a sharp dagger. I will plunge it right into your heart as you sleep peacefully. I will drink your blood. I will eat your liver raw. That way I will blend you, burn you, into my blood and flesh.

His reply, written in an impeccable hand, arrived in a few days:

> I am anguished, too. Would like to see you.

I set off immediately. I don't remember all the lies I told my husband. I've been open with you. I don't care for honesty when love and this ascetic are involved. I'll betray everyone—my children, my husband, my family, you, this whole world... I'll be cruelly disloyal.

Just as I was setting out, my younger daughter cried for something. I paid no heed. My older daughter fretted. That too escaped my attention. My husband looked gloomy. I didn't bother about that. I'm helpless. I cannot but go. All these folk, they are the business of this birth alone. He isn't like that. He's the ceaseless flow that links births past and forthcoming. My taproot.

I reached his house in the evening. It was a full moon night. The dusk lay all around me tranquil, silent. The moonlight fell upon his garden. Everywhere you looked, flowers were in bloom, white-clad and scented.

He had lit an oil lamp on the veranda and was reading something in its light. I pushed open the tile-roofed door. He looked up, anxious, hearing it creak. He saw me and set his reading aside. He stood up, leaning on the wall. He stood there gazing at me, arms behind his head.

That night I bathed in the river. He stood guard on the bank, with a lit lantern. The river was clear and cool. He picked the kaitha flowers for me. I lined my eyes with kohl for him. I braided my hair. We walked through the fields upon which the moonlight lay scattered. We sat on the path, in the middle of the fields, dipping our legs in the water. The moon shone bright upon the tangled tresses of the sky. The frogs croaked aloud. The green ones, memories from our past births. We listened carefully, silent. I was hurting inside and outside, a hard pain. My legs gave way when we began walking back. He held me.

We lit lamps in the serpent grove. We sat brushing against each other beneath the njaaval tree, looking at the lit lamps, at the swaying vines, at the birds drifting into slumber. Njaaval fruit fell like rain in the breeze. Then we talked.

He talked of his childhood. About his deceased parents, friends, romance in college, the early rigours of the ascetic life. I told him of my house. About my south-facing window, my river, my room, the breeze I trapped in it, of how I danced to the breeze clad in my silken skirt, the one with the golden brocade border. I kept eating the njaaval berries. My lips turned a dusky blue. He lifted my face to the moonlight. He kissed me. His lips turned dusky blue too.

The moonlight, the njaaval tree, the wet, withered leaves. The terrible pain. The pain of desire. This is the most painful part of this love. The touch-me-not clumps on the ground. Thorns fallen off a thorny tree. The sharp stones. The harder we embraced, the harder the ache. The njaaval berries were bruised, crushed. Their juice smeared my wound; it ached again.

'I remember now,' he said... 'For some time we were both bluebirds. You had a yellow spot on your beak.'

'And afterwards, for a long while we were fish. You had red spots on your tail...' I said.

'Weren't we sandal trees once? Didn't my roots entwine with yours under the soil?'

'After that we were stars…'

'And what are we now?'

He was sad.

Snakes, I consoled him. Snakes whose mouths and tongues had turned dusky blue from njaaval berries. We looked at each other vengefully. We hissed aloud. Fought with our venomous fangs. We struck each other with our tails and heads.

At dawn, beneath the tree, the njaaval berries lay crushed. Both of us turned deep blue, a dusky hue. He became mine. Defeated. Weak. But a slave. I found the answer to my question—Who am I? His owner. His mistress. His soul. He was completely mine. His eyes existed upon my image. His long, curly tresses existed for me to run my fingers through. His long beard, to graze my breasts. His fingers, to caress me. His chest, for me to rest my head upon. His neck, for me to bite, again and again. His life, for me to wound. His birth, to give me pleasure. I was half of him, the man in me. He was half of me, the woman in me. Two souls, intertwined. Two beings who'd sought each other through many births.

We were in ecstasy. I dug my nails into him. Bit and tore at his body. He received me tenderly and with pleasure. We laughed the whole night. In the morning we made rice gruel and chutney and ate from the same bowl. The ascetic told little jokes and light tales; he sang love songs. He spoke of my tresses, the colours that suited me. Of the son I might bear him. We delighted together in his frolic. We took pride in the quickness of his mind. Hoped that he reposed now in my womb, his tiny spine as delicate as a silken thread, his little brain, the size of a mustard seed. He pressed his face to my womb and gave our son a name. We laughed. I kissed him till he was exhausted.

It was now time for me to leave. We sagged. Our smiles faded. The pain rushed back. That moment, when I looked into his eyes to bid goodbye. His eyes. His deep eyes. Pain, tenderness, desire. Terrible loss. That's how I'll remember him on my deathbed. He too will remember my face from that moment. Maybe for many births. You do not know how we embraced at the parting moment. Surely, no woman has ever embraced a man like that. I didn't embrace him with my body. I held him with my soul. He replied with his soul. Our bones were crushed; our flesh was bruised. We melted into each other. Never can we embrace like this again. For we will never meet again. Never will we hold each other. Never will we spend the night together like this.

We will meet again, perhaps, in our next birth. Then too, I will slither like this. Over trees, and hills, over leaves and rocks. I'll seek him, slithering. Find him.

Then too, he will resist me, like now. He will try to push me away, to hate me. In the end, he will collapse from my bite.

Then too we will mate like now. And part, our hearts torn asunder.

Even if we part, my blood will long to blend with his.

~

I can't bear it. I am worn out. Body and soul, both are wounded. Memories. I've loved, loved, my blood vessels are clogged. I'm ageing fast. I'm becoming an old woman. My heart beats heavy each time, strained and worn. Each time, his name booms out. Each time, my eyes blink in pain. I see his face. Truly, I can't bear it. I'm worn out, trying to stop the immense Ganga in mid-air from falling. The river Ganga has to fall upon the earth. My eyes smart, not seeing him. My ears tingle, missing his voice. My fingers, my lips, this whole body, my blood, my heart, brain... without him, I writhe in smouldering pain.

I told you. Life experience needs honesty. Honesty has no need for morality. At night when my husband approaches me all aroused, I turn away, pretending I have a migraine. I sit transfixed, forgetting myself, as I prepare to sew a button on my older daughter's dress. As I sit beside my younger daughter's sickbed tending to her feverish body, I remember the wound on my left leg where he touched me first.

'What are you thinking about?' my husband asks me, sometimes.

'Nothing...' I say, with an attempt at a smile.

I dress in silk saris for my husband. Wear jasmine in my hair. Darken my eyes with kohl. Put colour on my lips. We go together to dinner parties and on vacations. We discuss the girls' future. On more settled nights, when he comes close, I may even let him do it.

My husband, my children, my house, my servants, my marble floors, my orchids, my anthurium...my outer skins growing tight. I stifle and gasp, for him.

I have never gone to that house afterwards. He wasn't there

anyway. He was sent to some ashram in Kashi or Haridwar. We never wrote to each other. I do not know where he is. I don't want to know, either. My love was a languid serpent of tremendous venom. It lay in wait for him, biding its time. He came. He trod on its hood. Made it into Takshaka, Kaliya, Anantha. He received it, and left. I will imagine him as a mendicant. In countries I do not know, traversing paths I'm ignorant of. Mountain passes clad in the white of snow. Paths paved with red sand. His feet reddened by the long walks. My form in his eyes. My love in his neck. In his arms, our son, who mirrors his face.

I can't take more. I can't say or write any more. Why, I've told you. This is not fiction, this is experience. An honest, burning sliver of experience. If it were fiction I could have turned it around. Could have said that he gave up asceticism, and I gave up a familial existence, and eloped. Or, I could have said that I apologized to my husband and remained a chaste wife for the rest of my days. But I'm helpless, this just happens to be a bit of life experience. A smouldering bit of life that can't be rewritten or denied. My love is like the house freshly on fire. Even in the downpour of separation, it blazes bright. Tongues of flame raise their hoods to the sky. This birth falls apart, seared, baked. Soon, another birth. The ascetic will come again. We will find each other again.

Once again, my deadly fangs will turn him blue—the deepest blue.

eight

~

# STOLEN

## AMRITA NARAYANAN

Parvathi, squat, generous-hipped, sweaty, is scraping seeds from the flesh of a papaya. She is working slowly, attentively, her brow furrowed in concentration as she strokes and probes with her curled brown fingers, her hands tracing slow ellipses to pull the glittering seeds from their sticky embrace with the sometimes red, sometimes orange flesh. At its wet centre, the fruit is exactly the colour of her santra-red sari and blouse.

Sitting across from her, Meenakshi, equally full of figure, still dusted with talcum powder and carrying the Mysore-sandal scent of her morning bath, is speaking. She is talking about papayas: how this year's bumper crop has dropped the prices and rendered accessible to everyone the exotic fruit that is usually the preserve of the wealthy; how, if plucked early, the hard, sour fruit makes for good pickling. It is mostly a monologue.

Parvathi keeps working as she listens, but doesn't say much; all through her chatter Meenakshi's eyes are riveted on her companion.

Though she is silent, Parvathi speaks with her body. Her thighs flex and twitch under the tightly wound cotton sari; a roll of flesh slick with sweat trembles just below the edge of her blouse. And now her feet flatten and dig into the tiled kitchen floor as she begins to juice the pile of lemon-halves she has sliced earlier. She twists and grinds the hard yellow rinds on the mound of the ancient glass juicer, until the pulp yields its tart juice into the waiting saucer. As she works, her breasts move within the enclave of her blouse, the cotton alternately caressing and chafing her nipples.

The cool black floor the two women sit on is not their usual working place: today, their mistress, Mrs Subramanium, has dispatched them to help her daughter, Sunita, prepare for one of her high-society lunches, and though the kitchen is smaller, and it takes the women longer to find the vessels that they need, both are grateful for the respite from Mrs Subramanium's stern demeanour. It is almost a holiday.

'Where is Uma?' Meenakshi mutters to herself. She knows that if Uma, Sunita's own maid, does not show up this morning, it will fall to her to pick up the girl's cleaning tasks, with Parvathi at once chef and sous chef. The consternation Meenakshi feels distracts her from Parvathi's rocking buttocks and her hands that are deftly massaging the last of the lemons. She stands up and looks around the kitchen in dismay as the morning's sensuality seems to fade and she is reminded of the drudgery that kitchen work can be when performed under stress.

Although she is oblivious to the precise nature of Meenakshi's thoughts, Parvathi senses a soupçon of irritation has crept into the other woman's body, where before there was a languid stillness. She looks at Meenakshi standing, tapping her foot, and then instinctively, and without knowing why, she stands up and places the weight of her own foot on the tapping one, stilling it and instantaneously reclaiming the sensual atmosphere of the kitchen.

Meenakshi puts a kilo of potatoes to boil on the gas stove, and Uma enters the kitchen to the screams of the pressure cooker.

In her bedroom, Sunita, dressed in an emerald-green silk tunic—her final choice after an hour of looking-glass trial and debate—falls back on her bed and turns on the television, flipping channels till she finds something to hold her interest: a nature show about the mating habits of lions. Transfixed, she watches as the male lion brings himself and his partner to orgasm in what seems like a very frantic few seconds. If the television could gaze back at her it might see her thighs roll inwards and her pubis lift, but as it is, there are no witnesses to Sunita's momentary arousal, the tiniest unfurling of her sex. She doesn't notice it herself. Then the thighs relax, the sacrum sinks, the moment passes.

Sunita switches the television off, briefly consults the clock and then heads down to the kitchen to check on lunch preparations, making a mental note to ask Uma to restore her room to its customary order after the meal.

In the kitchen, the sight of the counter strewn with coriander—Uma has left the partially de-leafed herb there to take her second bathroom break of the morning—annoys Sunita intensely. 'Ippodhaan chutney panna aarambichirukkiyaa?' she demands. 'Samosa filling readyaa?

'Uma yenna time vanthaa?' Meenakshi snaps to attention and scurries around, propelled by the pitch of Sunita's voice. 'Juice aarambichchacha? Modhalai juice pannu.'

Parvathi continues to chop the boiled potatoes into tiny cubes, unaffected by the sudden commotion. Her unconcern, bordering on disdain, angers Sunita, but she finds herself unable to lash out at the woman.

Instead, she snaps, 'And where is Uma?'

Uma bustles into the kitchen just then with a triumphant announcement: 'Juice is ready, madam. Fridge-la irukku.'

Sunita opens the fridge and bends over to peer in. The juice that Parvathi had squeezed from the limes has been transformed into a frosty affair with ice, sugar and mint leaves. The cubes of diced papaya have gone into a salsa prepared from a recipe she had pulled off the internet. Sunita sighs in relief, and something in the way her shoulders relax under the green silk makes Uma walk up and stand behind her mistress. She leans forward to point out the chutneys that are also ready and poured into the green ceramic bowls reserved for guests, and as she does so, her soft belly fits perfectly into the curve of Sunita's lower back, and her breasts rest on the bump of Sunita's upper back.

The ringing of a phone breaks the moment and Sunita straightens up sharply, bumping into Uma. By the time she reaches her cell phone, charging on the bookshelf in the corridor, it has stopped ringing and she stares at it, unable to decide whether or not to return the call from a number she does not recognize.

Uma stands in the kitchen doorway watching the other woman, seized by how similar their shapes are. When Sunita finally looks up, another moment of wordless understanding passes between them.

The phone rings again, and habit trumps instinct: Sunita says roughly to the woman in whose presence she has just felt herself unfolding, 'What do you want?'

I want to keep looking at you, Uma says with her eyes, refusing to avert them or respond with words to Sunita's attempt at reasserting the hierarchy between them.

Sunita looks away and picks up the phone. It's her mother. Uma doesn't look away. As she watches Sunita transform into a schoolgirl talking to her Amma, one hand on her left breast, as if checking her heartbeat, she is reminded of an afternoon two summers ago. She had walked into the bedroom to clean it and found Sunita before the dressing table, trying on new bras. In the mirror, Uma had seen a pair of chai-coloured breasts topple out as Sunita peeled off a flesh-coloured bra to try on a lacy grey-and-black one. Uma had never seen a bra like that, one that cupped Sunita's breasts with the gentleness of a sensitive lover, that did not pull them up tightly like the stiff white bras Uma herself wore.

She had also noticed how similar their breasts were: firm yet supple, coloured like they were brewed from the same batch of tea leaves, and topped with identical dark nipples, the colour of areca nuts. Even the space between Sunita's breasts matched her own perfectly: a canal just wide enough for a man's hardness.

The object of Uma's reverie, meanwhile, is rapidly and busily checking off items on the lunch list, responding to her mother's directives like an anxious obstetric-medical intern who, having delivered their very first baby, must make sure the creature is intact: yes ten toes, yes ten fingers, yes two areolae, yes a fold of skin between the legs that curves out and then in…

Hours later, it seems like no time has passed, except that now Uma is exhausted—sitting on her haunches, her sari hoisted up to her knees, its folds bunched between her sweaty, tired thighs. She's watching Sunita on the phone with her mother again, in the aftermath of the party. This time it is Uma who is counting. She's calculating that it will take Sunita exactly five more minutes to render the post-mortem of the afternoon to her mother, another ten to fetch the hundred-rupee tips she will give Parvathi and Meenakshi as they leave, and then, perhaps, just two minutes more before she will ask Uma to make her a fresh cup of tea and come up to her room. About seventeen minutes in all. And then, maybe—who knows? Uma has a brief vision of her face buried between Sunita's damp thighs.

But something different is going on today. On the phone, Sunita is protesting. 'No, Amma, not necessary.' But Mrs Subramanium always has her way, and Uma watches the daughter give in and say, 'Okay, okay, I will ask Parvathi for a massage, and yes, no oil on the head in the evening. I understand.' And then Sunita is calling for Parvathi and Parvathi is on the phone with Mrs Subramanium saying, 'Yes, madam, ah Dhanwantram thailam irukku, madam. Cheri, madam, okay, madam.'

When she understands what is about to happen, Uma's heart sinks. Suddenly, she is more exhausted than she had been after she cleared up the mess of the afternoon's lunch party. As the disappointment washes over her she hates herself, a top-worker, trained only to wash dishes and wipe floors, incapable of reading the labels on the bottles of Ayurvedic oil that Mrs Subramanium buys at Ayur Vaidya Shala and has chauffeur-delivered to her daughter. The hopelessness churns up from the pit of her stomach to the centre of her chest, and she can barely hear Sunita asking if she could stay until after the massage, because Parvathi will need someone to help her wipe down the oily rubber sheets and clear the massage table.

'Just rest and I'll call you when we are done,' Parvathi says kindly to Uma as Sunita tips Meenakshi, who is bone-tired and relieved to be leaving but cannot resist casting one last, longing look at Parvathi's wide buttocks.

Parvathi begins to prepare the double boiler in which she will warm the oil for the massage.

Uma is watching through the keyhole. At first she can only see Parvathi—drawing the heavy curtains so that the room is in darkness, lighting the fat, orange-scented candle that sits beside the massage table, and then waiting, patiently, for Sunita to emerge from the bathroom. Sunita comes out wrapped in a Sarthy towel—one of those thin, mill-made affairs that absorb so much water they are soaked after one wipe—a superfluous covering because she must shed it almost immediately so that Parvathi can help her with the massage langoti, a thin piece of muslin that Sunita will pass between her legs and fasten around her waist just to cover the dark triangle between her thighs.

Mesmerized by Sunita's naked body, by the breasts that are testimony to their twinship, Uma bends further towards the keyhole. Were the women inside the room to look back at her, through the door, they would see the sensual curve of Uma's own breasts, optimally exposed at that angle, sweat pools gathering at either edge of her pink choli, and beads of perspiration sliding down to her navel.

Sunita sits on a stool and Parvathi begins with long, gentle strokes on her angular neck and shoulders. Her skin receives the oil gratefully, like a thirsty man receiving water. The buzz of the afternoon's conversation is ringing through Sunita's head. Her friends had been talking about men: how today's men were becoming more sensitive, less patriarchal, but still had a long way to go. She had been unable to focus on the little fragments of conversation that spiralled up from every corner of the room, torn as she was between wanting to be the perfect hostess that her mother would have wished her to be and wanting to participate in the happy chatter. But now, Parvathi's skilful massaging begins to calm her down.

Parvathi asks Sunita to lie on her belly on the massage table. Her strokes grow even longer, re-establishing for Sunita the reality of her body. She finds she can make more sense of the afternoon now, and as she does she wonders why so many of these ladies' lunches revolve around the decisions of their men: hers and hers and hers. Or their own decisions made without the knowledge or the approval of their men. Or their decisions to live without men. There seemed to be nothing outside the kingdom of men; even the space inside the head of every woman there appeared to be the kingdom of some man, or a few men.

'Saapaadu nalla irundhudha?' Parvathi asks, as she runs her hands up and down Sunita's back, and then her arms: from the shoulders down to her fingers, then up again, her thumbs grazing the sides of Sunita's breasts, not furtively but with confidence.

'Yes, the food was good,' says Sunita reassuringly, and then a sudden need to confide makes her say: 'Ellarum aambalai pathiye pesinaanga.' Parvathi is moved at being allowed in so close. She shuts her eyes for a second, picturing herself talking with the group of smartly dressed and perfumed women at lunch. Parvathi does not know what comes over her then, for she says: 'Eppovum appadithaan! It's always like that, every woman talking about men. Don't we have cunts after all? Kadaseela aambalai paththeethaan paesuvom ellaam.'

Is that what it comes down to? Even as Sunita asks herself the question, the firm pressure of Parvathi's fingers on her inner thigh reminds her of something she has forgotten all day. She thinks better of pursuing the conversation, surrendering instead to the energy being pushed towards the place that Parvathi has just named. Then she gives herself over completely into feeling the one place that her mother has never given her any instructions about—except to cover it, close it, keep it tightly locked.

For the first time in a long while, Sunita allows herself to sink into the smell of herself. And then, slowly and deliberately, she distinguishes her own smell from the trifold scent of the Dhanwantram oil and two sets of armpits—hers and Parvathi's. Then, as Parvathi's fingers probe her flesh more urgently, she begins to recognize two Parvathi smells. The first comes from her unshaved armpits, sweaty after the day's labour.

And then there's the other Parvathi smell—unmistakeably the smell of cunt, slightly tangy, perhaps a little metallic, and carrying in it a whiff of damp earth.

Where do I remember that from, wonders Sunita, and even as she thinks about it Parvathi is rubbing more oil, her body is getting heavier and each stroke begins to separate her thoughts, allowing her to luxuriate in each of them individually. She begins to focus on one particular thought, which grows from the encouragement, like a fondled phallus. She remembers the smell. She remembers it rising from between her own legs the first time she climbed up into the loft of her parents' bedroom using the window grill as a foothold, looking in those black-and-white cabinets for Sidney Sheldon novels, which she flipped through until she found the words that had drawn her to that dark and secret place, words that released exactly this smell right there in her body, and released the moisture that accompanied it, this smell, and the sweetness that flooded her being when she rubbed the source of the smell—as she had done that day for the first time and brought her fingers to her mouth afterwards to taste.

Parvathi is massaging up from her ankles now, up past the back of her knees to the inside of her thighs and Sunita is wet but Parvathi is business-like. When Parvathi's thumbs come dangerously close to the langoti the second time Sunita absolves herself of the supervisory responsibility she took so seriously in the kitchen, thrusting the onus upon Parvathi and feeling quite sure that the maidservant can be counted upon to check herself. Just in time, each time.

Parvathi moves her thumbs in crescent-moon part circles that start at the back of Sunita's upper thigh and find their way slowly to her inner thigh. She barely touches the thin muslin that guards the lips between Sunita's legs before she lifts off and starts all over again at the outer thigh, each time advancing closer and very slightly deeper into the folds of the langoti. Sunita's eyes are firmly shut, and even as it occurs to her that she might be soaking the langoti with her juices, the thought is erased by the motion of Parvathi's kneading now on her buttocks, down and across, up and across and then in gentle circles around her sacrum.

Sunita can smell her own juices now, and as Parvathi straddles her to finish massaging her upper back, Sunita finds that if she loosens her belly, the weight of Parvathi's buttocks on her own, and the long, searching strokes that are now being applied from lower to upper back, create a delicious sensation in her cunt. As her pelvis jams into the weathered rubber mat that is on top of the massage table, subtle but nevertheless perceptible movements allow her to reap the harvest of oil that has collected in the mat from months of use—providing a complementary lubricant to the juices that are now matting the hair of her cunt. Just as she is beginning to pant a little, teeth grinding, mouth determinedly shut, stomach beginning to spasm, Parvathi suddenly stops.

Sunita is in an agony that could bring her to the verge

of tears in minutes unless she finds meaning in this moment. 'Yenna aachu?' Parvathi laughs softly. 'Please turn over, madam.' Motionless, Sunita waits till the hardness in her clitoris subsides, feeling the wail in her throat that she dare not release. In the stillness she accepts the loss of the place she had been visiting when Parvathi's movements stopped. Then, hoping that in the candlelight Parvathi will not notice anything, Sunita turns over.

The slight breeze of the November afternoon causes her to shiver slightly as she rolls her hips up and open to expose first her soaked, langoti-sheathed pubis, then the line of her waist and breasts bearing erect nipples as she lies down on her back and waits. Parvathi begins the dorsal massage at the legs, long lines addressing the points of pressure from thigh to toe, followed by a gentle pummelling and slapping that render first her right leg and then her left completely free of tension.

Her ankles give way and her feet fall to either side. Parvathi climbs on to the massage table and straddles Sunita's hips without putting her weight on them. The folds of her sari drop gently down, meeting the moisture of the langoti, and the folds of skin just beyond the paper-thin moist cotton skein. She massages Sunita's belly first, using her whole palm to rub across her waist in one direction then the other, eventually pressing her fingertips around Sunita's belly button to release the knots of tension there, the undigested pieces of lunch.

It's probably too soon after lunch to have a massage, Sunita thinks, the thought disappearing as soon as Parvathi pours a tiny quantity of oil into Sunita's belly button.

Another day she may have been squeamish, but today she feels no ticklishness, and her clitoris hardens in response to the delicate circular motion Parvathi is now using to pleasure the grooves of her navel that in turn sends electric ripples all the way down into her cunt. She moans very softly, and the thought that tells her to conceal the sound is wiped clean by the sensation of warm oil now being trickled on to her breasts. Sunita holds back a scream of relief; she feels Parvathi's hands grasp each of her breasts and hold them firmly for a few seconds before beginning to massage them one by one, in broad, circular motions that encompass the whole breast. She sighs audibly as Parvathi works on her heavy breasts, pushing them from one side to another and watching how they fall as if admiring ripe fruit. If she were to look at Sunita's face instead of her breasts Parvathi would notice that her employer's daughter has ever so slightly opened her eyes.

The sight of Parvathi astride her, one breast in each hand, the line between her own neck and breasts exposed, glittering with sweat, pumps every nerve ending in Sunita's clitoris alive, bringing a fresh rush of dew to the petals of her cunt. In little crawling movements, like an insect making its way up a mud-hill, Parvathi is pinching the flesh of Sunita's breasts in smaller and smaller circles and ending in a very slight pinch to the nipple that causes Sunita to grasp either edge of the massage table tightly and whimper softly.

It is when Parvathi is repeating this movement for the third time, this edging up the breast, exploring and pinching, that she suddenly becomes aware of Sunita's arousal. She is struck by the pathos of the moment, the drama of power role reversal, but when she moves it is not from the munificence of one bestowing a favour.

There is not a second of planning, not an iota of forethought, but a boldness that can only come from an animal sense of knowing. Forbidden, in the rules of massage that she had studied that summer when Mrs Subramanium had decided that Parvathi would be a cheaper substitute for the Kerala-trained Ayurvedic masseuse, is pulling, and this is what Parvathi now does: she gently but firmly pulls both Sunita's nipples simultaneously, one in each hand, as she rocks back and forth, now sitting on her haunches, one foot on either side of Sunita's hips. The thick folds of her sari collect between her own thighs, and gently stimulate her via the movement while simultaneously, because the heavy cotton material is long enough—a six-yard Mangalgiri cotton inherited from Mrs Subramanium herself—it licks the folds of Sunita's langoti and pubis, creating an electrical impulse that along with the pulling of her nipples cause Sunita to break out in a sweat.

There is now no question of opening her eyes and also no turning back or denying what is happening.

Parvathi is rocking and Sunita gives in, allowing her buttocks to slightly lift off the table so her cunt can fully meet the folds of Parvathi's sari. The friction increases. Perceiving this shift Parvathi drops on to her knees and slides down the mat, then lowers her hips further so that her own cunt is grazing Sunita's and her hands are on either side of Sunita's shoulders for support. She is moving like a man now and the folds of cloth between the two women's cunts are soaking. The effort of being silent is now far greater than the risk of making a sound, and an unmistakable panting and grunting breaks out. At the keyhole, Uma is sliding up and down the door almost exactly imitating Parvathi's movement. She is unable to hold back her screams but she has the thoughtfulness to scream noiselessly, mouth open, shoulders thrown back. She has formed the folds of her own sari into a thick cylindrical structure mimicking the thickness and firmness of a man's cock and she is rotating her hips round and round in circles, grinding them into the roll of cloth while she tightens her grip on the door handle and watches through the crack in the panelled wood.

Sunita is coming hard and intensely. My pussy is in ecstasy, she screams into her own heart because she knows she must not scream out loud. Her mouth is open and her face covered in sweat; her eyes are still closed, but Parvathi knows from the way her hips suddenly lift up off the massage table, the way her buttocks are tensing, toes pointing and her grip tightening on the table, to move just enough to bring her to one more shudder and to then seamlessly glide into a neck massage.

Uma too has released, panting, satiated. Eyes finally closed, she rests her forehead against the door oblivious to the rectangular stain of sweat that immediately appears where she touches it. Parvathi herself is not spent but she is less concerned with her own pleasure this afternoon than with fully and completely satisfying Sunita. Getting off the massage table she turns her back to Sunita and begins to deeply work the tissues of Sunita's belly, pressing downwards, releasing the air created by the orgasm and readying Sunita's body for what she will do next.

I don't want this to stop. I don't want this to stop.

The six-word ritornello that is echoing in Sunita's head is a direct communication from her cunt and, without words, Parvathi has heard it, and now her palms are together in a prayer position, ten fingers touching as she slides the edge of her folded hands from Sunita's navel down towards her pubis, then quickly lifting up and beginning again at the navel, pressing the edge of the hands into the belly and pushing down once more, first slowly and then rapidly. When she intuits Sunita's readiness by the curve of her now slightly relaxed buttocks she stops and begins to untie Sunita's langoti.

It's over, thinks Sunita and the disappointment falls like dead weight into every inch of her being. The fog of her depression descends so quickly and thickly that she does not at first feel what Parvathi is doing: she is releasing the back of the langoti so that she can manipulate with both her hands the cloth that is between Sunita's legs. In another minute she is pulling on either end of the muslin with the motion of a milkmaid, and Sunita's whole cunt is dancing in glee, as the slippery muslin soaked with the fragrance of her juices wafts up to her such that she does not know what is more pleasurable, smell or touch, and she is coming again, this time thrashing and bouncing her hips up and down so hard that her upper body rises up off the table before falling back down.

'Geyser on panirku, ma,' says Parvathi announcing the readiness of the bath and brushing the hair from the younger woman's face. Sunita opens her eyes as she always does at the end of her massage, and thanks Parvathi out loud, gratitude shining in her eyes like stars in those places where city lights do not drown the magnificence of the night sky. Parvathi nods and then leaves the room, turning the doorknob quietly but nearly bumping into Uma as she opens the door.

She grabs her fiercely and for a second Uma thinks Parvathi is going to hit her although she can't understand why: after all, her insolence is no less than anyone else's. But it is not violence that Parvathi is craving and for a minute she contemplates Uma, holding her arm in a vice-like grip, breathing her in and smelling the sandwich of cilantro, onions, armpit and cunt.

Inside, Sunita is allowing herself one more minute of bliss, a marvelling at the miracle of her own body before she slides off the massage table, tiptoes into the bathroom and turns on the shower. The sound of cascading hot water enters the room and fills it. Outside, Uma is frozen in Parvathi's clutch. Stuck, she has a moment of enlightenment in the arms of her captor: it is she who longs to strike Parvathi, the capillaries of her soul are dilated with jealousy, she has been watching Sunita hungrily for months, and the rapture of seeing her beloved pleasured before her eyes is now overruled by the awareness of its cost: something precious was lost to her and her rage at her loss is immense. She grabs Parvathi in a wrestler's hold, locks her leg around the older woman's and pushes her to the ground. It is then that she smells Sunita on Parvathi and she half-yelps, half-shrieks: the sound of commingled violence and lust. Nostrils flaring, chest exploding, she follows the trail of the scent, ruthlessly pinning body parts as she moves, and this time it is Parvathi who is immobilized, as Uma's hands rip her sari and petticoat, and her head enters the opening she has created, grunting and panting, feverishly fumbling and, eventually, finding the destination her nose and tongue seek.

nine

~

# LOVE REVOLUTION*

## IRA TRIVEDI

My dadaji was a great one for aphorisms. I will never forget one he told me on my twenty-first birthday. He said I should get married quickly because 'women are like balls of dough. If they sit around for too long they harden and make deformed chapattis.' My grandfather believed that a good marriage was like a perfectly round chapatti and to achieve this perfection, the dough had to be supple, fresh and young. It has been nearly seven years since then, and now at twenty-eight, I am unequivocally, by Dadaji's standards, a hardened, deformed, inedible roti.

My marriage has been talked about since the day I turned eighteen. My first solo trip with my grandfather was to the Vishwanath (an avatar of Shiva) temple in Varanasi where I was made to perform a puja to acquire a good husband, with Dadaji supervising the proceedings.

*Extracted from *India in Love*

Of all the gods in the Hindu pantheon, Lord Shiva is the easiest to please as he is known to fulfil a supplicant's desires sooner than the rest of the gods. To appease my mother and to absolve myself of the consequences of any negative action in my past lives that could delay my marriage, I performed fasts for sixteen consecutive Mondays—the holy day of Lord Shiva.

Unfortunately the fasts did not work as my family had wished, and I remained unmarried. Ten years ago, I would have been considered way beyond my sell-by date, but today it is no longer unthinkable for an Indian woman to be single at twenty-eight.

I am stuck in the liminal space between the old and the new, the past and the present, the East and the West. I am a product of the hubris of this new India. When I was younger, ever since I could understand the concept of marriage, I was told that I must get married to a suitable boy: a Hindu, belonging to my Brahmin caste, preferably within the Kanyakubj sub-caste. Love, attraction, or even liking was not a priority. The first time that my grandfather saw my grandmother was on the day of their wedding. They were married for sixty-five years till my dadiji passed away two years ago. My parents saw each other in black-and-white photographs, and then met twice with their entire families present before they got married. As a kid, I listened confused and dumbfounded as I was bombarded with tales of the genetic superiority and mental purity of Brahmins. My uncle's inter-caste love marriage in the 1970s to my Punjabi aunt was narrated as a dark tale disguised as warning. All this was forgotten the day I left my parents' home to go to college in the US where I quickly, almost desperately, started dating all the wrong sorts of boys. Once that happened, it seemed weird to enter into an arranged marriage. Just like with my boyfriends, it seemed natural to want to get to know my husband-to-be intimately, to understand his mental make-up, his notions of love and hardship, his life before we met, what he liked to eat, what his preferred sleeping position was, and *only then* arrive at a decision for the commitment of a lifetime.

With the country's changing outlook on relationships, even my traditional family has begun to rethink their views on marriage. Just ten years ago, my elder sister, Ishani, was married at the age of twenty-one. A marriage broker would probably call her wedding an 'arranged-cum-love' or 'introduction marriage', a quaint hybrid of the traditional arranged marriage and a love match. In Ishani's case, my parents identified an appropriate boy—a well-educated, tall, fair boy of the same caste who was a doctor in the US. He was a perfect match for their twenty-one-year-old engineer daughter. Ishani had little option but to marry that suitable Brahmin boy; it would have been unacceptable for her to marry out of caste.

They remain happily married. A decade after Ishani's arranged marriage, my younger sister had a love marriage to Rahul, whom she met at work. My parents were thrilled that she had found a partner of her choice. Unlike in Ishani's case, Rahul's caste was a bonus, not the major criterion. Rahul is fortunately a Brahmin (though his family is from Kashmir, and speak a different language from ours, eat meat and have their own customs). My parents have changed with time as they see the children of their friends and family members marry out of caste, and even people of other nationalities; they have accepted that times are different, and caste no longer holds the supreme importance that it once did. Even people as traditional as my grandfather, the longest serving president of the Brahmin Samaja, known the world over for his prowess in getting young people married, is coming to terms with love and inter-caste marriage. On a recent visit to his native village, Etawah, he was overheard telling an old classmate from his college days how convenient it was that these days children found their own partners and parents/relatives no longer had to run door to door with their daughters' birth charts.

∽

For centuries, marriage has been the mainstay of Indian culture. In the institution of arranged marriage is embedded the idea of a lifetime of commitment—to each other and to family. Today, this is fast changing, and it is estimated that over 30 per cent of urban India chooses to marry for love. Yet arranged marriage continues to be the preferred option in the country.

Let's look at why arranged marriage has remained so important.

A historical overview of arranged marriage suggests that it serves primarily as a means of solidifying alliances between families. Although this is a common feature of marriages across cultures, it takes specific valences in the socio-historical context of India. India's unique joint family social structure, in which men live with their parents, brothers, and wives, can be traced to the Vedas. Although urbanization and migration (both domestic and international) are changing Indian families, most families have adapted the joint family structure (for example, with one brother and his wife living with the parents, with children sharing finances with their families beyond marriage) rather than adopting nuclear family structures that characterize Euro-American unions. Elderly parents continue to rely on sons for support, which also reinforces marriage as the concern of the extended family; only 1 per cent of the elderly population lives in old-age homes. In this context, arranged marriages are particularly important because they ensure the well-being of the entire family rather than just of the individual, and elaborate wedding ceremonies again reflect this heightened significance. For example, in Mughal times, marriages fulfilled political alliances between different ruling lineages, including between Hindu rajas and Mughal rulers.

Sources on Mughal marriages suggest that royal marriages were particularly important to the continuation of both family and political rule (which were united due to hereditary rule) and that rulers were most concerned with marriages in times of political instability.

The caste system too heightened the importance of arranged marriage. The Hindu caste system was traditionally based on employment categories and that demanded marrying within one's caste. Throughout history marriage has been used to bolster caste and intra-caste cohesion. For example, the Hindu revival movement in the mid-twentieth century included caste conferences that called for endogamy in order to strengthen the caste system.

British colonial rule saw the new rulers interfering with and moulding laws governing marriage as part of their drive to codify and regularize the 'personal laws' of the various religious and caste groups in the country. Some of this impulse sprang from a genuinely fair-minded desire to organize the plethora of confusing strictures that governed marriage and society in the country, and some of it was rooted in an attempt to perpetuate the divide and rule philosophy that the British followed. The British also codified Hindu marriage laws according to Brahminic customs, including dowry. This resulted in the stringent adherence to endogamy within castes and religions, strengthening the system of the arranged marriage at the national level.

## LOVE IN THE TIME OF BOLLYWOOD

Though arranged marriage may seem to be a totally retrograde concept to many in the West, the reality is that up until the late eighteenth century, most societies around the world had arranged marriages where love developed *after* getting married to a suitable life partner, not before. Marriage was considered to be an economic and political institution, much too important to be left to the whims and passions of two young and inexperienced individuals. It was only in the late eighteenth century that the idea of marrying for love, based on the free will of two people began gaining strength. Today, the idea of marrying for love is so deep-set in most of the West, and even a large part of the East, that we tend to forget that it has only been about 200 years since men and women began to wrest control of their marriage from their families and the church.

Historian Stephanie Coontz in her excellent book, *Marriage, a History: How Love Conquered Marriage,* studies the marital patterns in North America and Europe. She concludes that marriage has changed more in the Western world in the previous thirty years than it has in the past three thousand. The 'love revolution' began in the US in the eighteenth century when the development of a market-driven economy led to the erosion of traditional social systems. Young people began accepting the radical idea that love should be the primary reason for marriage, and that they should be free to choose their own partners. Yet marriage continued to be of paramount importance as men and women were seen as fundamentally different beings, sexually and otherwise—the man was the provider while the woman was the nurturer. By the 1970s, the love revolution culminated with marriage losing its centrality in society and people stopped believing that marriage was a necessary step to lead fulfilling lives. After extensive research, Coontz specified four criteria that led to the breakdown of traditional marriage.

These four criteria are:

1. The belief that men and women are different in terms of sensibility, lifestyle and sexuality
2. The ability of society to regulate an individual's personal behaviour and punish them for nonconformity
3. The combination of women's economic dependence on men and men's domestic dependence on women
4. Unreliable birth control and fear of pregnancy

While Coontz's theory applies to the Indian scenario as much as it does to the US, the way it plays out is quite different. Though marriage in India continues to play an important role in people's lives, it is seeing a lot of change. The tradition of arranged marriage is breaking down as people choose to marry for love rather than for religious, caste, family or economic reasons. For the first time in thousands of years, India is going through a unique love revolution in which young people are taking the marriage decision into their own hands and choosing to marry for love. According to a study by the International Institute for Population Sciences and Population Council that conducted interviews with 51,000 married and unmarried young men and women from six states—Andhra Pradesh, Bihar, Jharkhand, Maharashtra, Rajasthan and Tamil Nadu—77 per cent of unmarried women think they should be able to take their own decisions about marriage.

Let's look at India's love revolution more closely by applying each of Coontz's points to the Indian scenario.

1) *The belief that men and women are different in terms of sensibility, lifestyle and sexuality*

The Victorian stipulations of the Raj-era that men and women are inherently different and should move in separate spheres are under attack. Till just a decade ago, single-sex Catholic convent schools were regarded as the height of educational excellence, attended by the children of the elite. Today, many of the premier schools and colleges in India's urban centres are co-educational. Likewise, as Gita Aravamudan points out in her book *Unbound: Indian Women at Work*, ever since Indian women began entering the workplace in significant numbers in the 1950s and 1960s, social attitudes towards them began changing in a number of ways. Men began wanting wives who were educated. After independence, new work opportunities came around which required men to move away from their hometowns and joint families. Without the support of a joint family, women were forced to leave their homes and undertake chores that their office-going husbands had no time for. As women left the confines of their homes, they discovered an attractive world and the advantages of economic freedom. A silent, almost unnoticed 'revolution' was occurring in the middle class and, suddenly, educated women were seen as financial assets by men. Women began entering the market force in large numbers as nurses, teachers, stenographers and bank clerks. These working women, exposed to industry, had higher aspirations for their daughters who grew up and took the work force by storm. By the 1970s women were working alongside their male counterparts in the corporate and public sectors.

With the opening up of the Indian economy in the 1990s, new avenues of employment presented themselves to women. These new opportunities were not segregated by sex and included positions in call centres, software companies, biotechnology and the new media. The autonomy of middle-class women transformed the traditional Indian family as girls were encouraged to get an education and a job. The Indian IT-BPO industry pioneered employment for women and, more than any other industry in the country, promoted the interests of women in the workplace. Today, the IT industry has a larger proportion of women employees as compared to other sectors. The coming together of men and women in the workplace, and their changing roles in society generally, has severely dented any existing notions that they are vastly different from each other.

2) *The ability of society to regulate an individual's personal behaviour and punish them for nonconformity*

The ability of family, relatives, government and neighbours to regulate personal behaviour is eroding quickly in India. There is an increasing pattern of migration where young people are moving away from their families to study and work, choosing to live alone in urban areas, free from family regulations and pressure. A 2010 McKinsey Global Institute study on 'India's Urban Awakening' predicts that 590 million people, about 40 per cent of the country's population, will live in cities by 2030, and 70 per cent of net new employment will occur in cities; up from 340 million in 2008 (30 per cent of the population).

The pattern of urbanization and migration has allowed for far more anonymity in personal life, and less penalization for personal choices, as young people live and operate far from the watchful eyes of their families, relatives or communities. Age-old institutions such as the village councils or khap panchayats that regulate individual and societal behaviour are slowly losing favour, particularly amongst the youth, who would rather move away from small towns and villages than suffer these stifling regulations.

The economic boom in India has resulted in the rise of national and multi-national companies, banks and other impersonal institutions that do not hire based on sex, caste, religion or marital status, making it easier than ever before to lead anonymous lives free from the pressures of family and society. Anonymity also increases with the help of technology. Gone are the days of trunk calls and surreptitious love letters. Cell phones have greatly increased the ability of the individual to control his/her fate and be freed from societal restraints.

3) *The combination of women's economic dependence on men and men's domestic dependence on women*

The dreams of the Indian woman are piercing through the walls of the kitchen and the living room, leaving behind rubble, glass and other debris. More women are working than ever before and becoming financially independent. The prevalence of women in the workplace is 30 per cent in metropolitan areas—with a 10 per cent increase in just the past year. According to a recent survey by the Centre for Work-Life Policy, more than 80 per cent of the women surveyed said they wanted top jobs and were prepared to work hard for them.

Women's income has also risen contributing to the 'girl power' economy. According to a recent survey by the Indian Market Research Bureau (IMRB) the average monthly income of women living and working in urban areas in India increased from ₹4,492 in 2001 to ₹9,457 in 2010. There has been a huge growth in savings accounts owned by women in the last few years—₹14 million in 2007 to ₹29 million in 2011, and also a 78 per cent growth in women credit card owners in the last four years.

The effect of consumerism too has been a game-changer for women. The marketplace is flooded with gadgets like microwaves, washing machines, ovens, etc. that have decreased the time and labour spent on household chores. Most middle-class households have a fridge and, increasingly, washing machines. Day-care centres and pre-schools have increased options for child-care; this is particularly important for women in urban nuclear families. The freedom of Indian women to make their own decisions has also increased, shaping marketing and branding trends. It is estimated that 'the percentage of women who made decisions about buying household durables like washing machines, refrigerators, cars, etc. has gone up from 15 per cent to 20 per cent in the last few years.'

Men too benefit from the easy availability of sophisticated white goods and are becoming less dependent on women. Bachelorhood has become easier than ever before, and even married men are beginning to take on more household responsibilities. A popular Indian chef, Sanjeev Kapoor, in an interview in *The Guardian* newspaper said, 'Twenty years ago if you said you cooked, people would ask what was wrong with you. Now it is the opposite.' Close to 49 per cent of the visitors to his website are male—a 20 per cent increase from just two years ago.

I observe too that many of the young working men that I come across prefer to eat a lunch of fast food—pizzas, burgers and sandwiches—rather than a meal cooked by mothers or wives.

Couples marry (and stay married) when the gains of marriage exceed the gains of being single. In the past, these economic gains would allow advantages to both partners and traditionally centred around women having an economic advantage at home doing household work, and men generating income by going to work (or working in the field). Today, this has changed, and much of what was once produced at home by women can be purchased or produced by men. Women, like men, can do income-generating work. This decreases the gains from marriage. At the same time, increasing leisure time and disposable income, along with the changing landscape of sexual relationships potentially raises the opportunity cost of being single. All in all, marriage is not as economically viable as it once used to be. Changes in tastes, technology, and institutional and legal environments have decreased gains from marriage.

4) *Unreliable birth control and fear of pregnancy*
Various studies show that once the fear of pregnancy disappears, women's sexual conduct becomes unconstrained and sex, particularly premarital sex, becomes freer. In India, abortion is legal and there are no social sanctions against the practice. Birth control is based on efforts largely sponsored by the Indian government as a measure for population control and contraceptive devices have been freely and openly available in India. Contraceptive usage has more than tripled—from being used by 13 per cent of married women in 1970 to 48 per cent in 2009. Over-the-counter birth control pills are cheaply and widely available.

Nandan Nilekani, in his book *Imagining India*, delves into the history of birth control in India. He writes, 'As the global panic around population growth surged, the Indian and Chinese governments began executing white-knuckle measures of family planning in the 1960s'. This reached its zenith in the mid-1970s with the announcement of the Emergency. Sanjay Gandhi made male sterilization his baby and the programmes he threw his weight behind were responsible for nearly eight million sterilizations, millions of them forced. A *New York Times* article from 1982 speaks about India's national birth control programmes launched by then Prime Minister Indira Gandhi:

> Prime Minister Indira Gandhi proclaimed February as 'family welfare month.' Billboards equating the 'small family,

> happy family,' were put up in every state, and radio programs advocated family planning.
>
> The major reason for the campaign is that India's census last year counted 684 million people, 12 million more than demographers had predicted. Subsidized birth control pills and condoms are being distributed, but most of the emphasis has been on sterilizations.
>
> Most of those turning up at the medical camps are women who receive $22 for submitting to a quick surgical closing of their Fallopian tubes. Men who get vasectomies are given $15. The difference in payments reflects the new emphasis on women as the key to family planning.

In India, there is a fifth factor that has aided the love revolution: Bollywood. Bollywood has been a major influence and in certain sections of society, the Indian family has become far more tolerant to the idea of love marriages with the dramatic rise in movies that show inter-communal or inter-class love stories. This has also become a frequent theme on sitcoms and reality shows on cable television. Cable television, with a penetration of 200 million, has also had a significant impact. From two channels in 1991, Indian viewers were exposed to more than fifty channels in 1996 because of new economic policies. Foreign channels imported foreign cultures and norms, and Western concepts of dating and love were unleashed on Indian minds. The simplicity and prudishness of the national channel Doordarshan was replaced by Star TV, MTV and a host of others, and American culture was served on the go to an entire generation.

To find out more about how India's love revolution is unique, I speak with author Stephanie Coontz, author of *Marriage: A History: How Love Conquered Marriage.*

'For better or for worse, the love match is here to stay,' declares Coontz. 'Whatever our own personal opinions are and whatever the strengths of the arranged marriage system may be, arranged marriage is not going to exist indefinitely in today's globalized world.'

In the West, the love revolution happened in two distinct steps. First, there was the development of market driven, individualistic nuclear families because of economic and social processes; as a consequence, the prevailing economic and social systems which were the means to exercise control over young people began to erode. This created an environment ripe for the love revolution to play out in its second stage—with rising female independence, new jobs, access to birth control, etc.

In India, though, everything is happening at the same time. The change in mindset that the family controls everything, the opening up of opportunities, the relaxation of social barriers, the creation of entertainment options, the easier mingling of the sexes, access to birth control—everything is being churned together in one unholy mix.

The one key difference is that in the West, by the second stage of the revolution, the ability of parents to control their children had been wiped out. That has not yet happened in India. Even though there is a trend of young people wanting freedom from parents, and wanting Bollywood style romantic liaisons, they are also getting much more pushback than Western young women and men ever got. There are still many hangovers in rural and even urban parts of India of the old system of social production and reproduction, so the tensions that the love revolution creates are going to be much higher in India than they were in the West.

I wonder how much of a role religion and the caste system have played in the Indian love revolution. Coontz explains, 'Religion and the caste system are all intertwined. In the West, religion was intertwined with the development of marriage, but the religion there reflected more individualizing tendencies that led to the early development of the market economy. There was less cultural, religious, and socio-economic support for marriage in the West than there ever was in India.'

Since arranged marriage is rooted in the major religions of the subcontinent such as Hinduism, Islam, Jainism, Sikhism and even Indian versions of Christianity and Zoroastrianism, and religion is such an important force in India, how is this going to change? Coontz replies, 'Throughout history, societies have adapted to social and economic change. Religious structures in a religion like Hinduism reflect a society where control over the young was important to reproduction because of the caste system. But Hinduism has always been evolving, and as the tide gets strong enough to turn it, religion will adapt. It won't happen exactly like the Western model, but it will adjust to allow freedom in conjunction with its traditions.'

∽

Over the past decade or so, the biggest change to India's love story has been that romantic love has become a legitimate basis to wed. This has become a common experience amongst the urban, educated middle-class Indians. Essential to this love story is a Western-style consumerism and today in novels, films and television serials alike, young couples fall in love over coffee and movie dates, in malls and in exotic Western locales.

The Bollywood movie today is the most telling aspect of how modern India sees love. Very often the hero and heroine exchange an English 'I love you' even as they fight for their romantic love against the wishes of their families.

Displays of love too have seen an interesting journey in Bollywood films. Earlier, the kiss was considered to be a Western pollutant, and censor boards, filmmakers and even audiences saw the absence of kissing as upholding Indian culture and tradition. Over the last decade, this prudery is slowly disappearing and the kiss has become a common feature of Bollywood movies. For example, veteran filmmaker Yash Chopra depicts a long kiss in *Mohabbatein* (2000), when earlier he did not have a kiss even between an adulterous couple depicted naked in a bedroom sequence (*Silsila*, 1981). Most recently, in late 2012, Shahrukh Khan, India's leading film star, who never kissed on screen for moral reasons, succumbed to public pressure and shared his first on-screen kiss with his co-star in the blockbuster *Jab Tak Hai Jaan*.

India has had a rich, spectacular romantic past, and love, kama, ishq, pyaar, mohabbat, call it what you will, has always been an integral part of our cultural and historical past. Love in India may have taken on different names, forms and meanings, but it is the importance that Indian culture has given to love that has lent it richness. It is ironic then that a country like India that has recorded, celebrated and presented love in such a variety of forms shuns the concept of romantic love in modern times. Although the stigma associated with romance and love is decreasing, in many parts of India, there is still a grave threat to lovers and the love match.

## THE LOVE COMMANDOS

When fiction bleeds into real life, the results are not as pretty, because as Kothari, Coontz, and numerous others point out, India is still far from ready to whole-heartedly embrace the concept of free love. This is where one of the unique by-products of this revolution has emerged: the Love Commandos.

I alight from an auto and traverse the narrow alleys of Paharganj, a central Delhi marketplace known for its cheap hotels and backpackers. 'Follow me' beckons the Commando who will show me the way to the central office of the Love Commandos. He walks slowly, but in the whirr of sounds, sights and people, I lose him. I struggle to find him in the maze-like ancient alleys of what was, in the eighteenth century, Delhi's principal grain market. Today, this is an urban marketplace, spilling over with people, automobiles and animals. I absorb the odours and bewildering sights and sounds as I walk past a shanty. I re-establish contact with my guide and follow him through a crowded market, past a shop featuring men's Lux Cozi underwear and another one where a pair of lime-green draw-string pajamas with an ice-cream-cone-print takes up prime display space. I walk past a stable, which holds twenty albino mares with fast-blinking pink eyes, some of them decked out in colourful wedding paraphernalia. These are wedding horses, traditionally meant to be white and female, on which the groom will ride on his wedding day. I cross a hole-in-the wall police station (so tiny that it has room only for one police officer, one chair, and a beat-up phone) which is in curious contrast to a 'Men's western saloon', a two-chair barber shop next door. The hulking Commando finally takes a left turn into a congested alley where an ancient woman with a shrivelled face is sitting on a cot peeling vegetables; another octogenarian next to her, wearing a pair of magnifying-glass-like spectacles is stringing together raakhis for the upcoming raksha bandhan festival—she gives me a toothless smile.

The Commando leads me into a decrepit one-room shanty, with uneven bruise-coloured walls, riddled with stains, scars and scribbles. He declares that this is the head office of the Love Commandos. The twenty-square-foot room is unventilated and has an unidentifiable odour. The floor is caked with dust and littered with several shoe-print-stamped loose papers. A stack of dirt-covered books lines the walls and wires sprout from many corners. The main points of interest in the room are a flat-screen monitor, a computer, a smut-covered printer and a blinking internet router. I am a little taken aback. The Love Commandos' website boasted a lot of media coverage, international and national, including the BBC, *The Guardian*, *The Times*, and a host of others. Most recently, they had been featured on the hugely popular television show *Satyamev Jayate,* hosted by Bollywood celebrity Aamir Khan. I would have imagined that they would be operating with more resources.

Taking up most of the office space is a corpulent Harsh Malhotra, who introduces himself as the Chief Coordination

Officer. Next to him is a petite Sanjoy Sachdev, the emerald-eyed Chairman of the Commandos. They are dressed for the interview in crisp, starched, white-linen kurta pajamas. A grimy plastic stool is dragged forward for me to sit on. A noisy air-cooler makes it difficult for me to hear what they have to say, but the electricity promptly goes off and that problem is solved. Candles are lit in the dark, windowless room even though it is bright and sunny outside.

On the night of Valentine's Day, 14 February 2010, Sanjoy Sachdev and Harsh Malhotra spent the night in jail. They had been arrested for protecting lovers against the wrath of right-wing Hindu groups. That night they decided to dedicate their lives to helping lovers and took the fate of India's young lovebirds into their own hands. To deal with the inordinate number of honour killings that had been taking place, they started Love Commandos, an organization dedicated to helping lovebirds flee their pursuers. Their ultimate goal was to eliminate honour killings from the Indian landscape. Love Commandos is Chairman Sanjoy's brainchild, and he speaks passionately and poetically about how love must be unequivocally protected.

'People used to think we were mad. They captured us and threw us in jail. Do you know how many Valentine's Days I have spent in jail? More than you have seen in your life!'

In a country with deep-seated traditions of patriarchy, casteism and family honour, falling in love across caste and community lines is difficult, and sometimes even life-threatening. Threats to the lives of lovers often come from their own families—families who believe they lose face in society by the romantic actions of their wayward kin and reports of honour killings of young lovers have become rather common in newspapers. These cases are often cloaked in obfuscation, with few legitimate sources and little evidence. In cases of inter-caste or inter-community romance, the risk of being killed is so great, especially in certain north Indian states, that the government has opened police shelters for runaway couples where they are offered protection against the brutality of their family members. 'The Punjab and Haryana High Court receives as many as 50 applications per day from couples seeking protection. This is a staggering tenfold rise from about five to six applications a day five years ago'.

Despite the menacing odds, love and longing in the small towns of India is increasing like never before. Young men and women are braving centuries of social resistance and daring to fall in love across caste lines. '[A]nnually around 984 Dalits marrying non-Dalits get protection orders in runaway marriages'. About eight to ten establishments in Chandigarh conduct marriage ceremonies to provide the required certificate of marriage to the couple and a marriage arranger in a temple claimed that a temple in Punjab had solemnized 1,500 marriages over the last five years.

The Love Commandos' main agenda is to rescue endangered couples from the wrath of families and bring them to the safety of their shelter in Delhi where they offer protection. Once the couples arrive at the shelter, Harsh and Sanjoy act as mediators, speaking with their parents, community leaders and politicians, negotiating terms and conditions for the return of the lovebirds to their homes. Sometimes they even perform marriage ceremonies for runaway couples. They tell me about several life-threatening missions that they have embarked on, in most cases to rescue the girl, who is forcefully held by her parents. I ask if I can accompany them on their next mission. They refuse, saying that my life would be under serious threat if I were to go with them. They point to the Commando who has led me here.

'He is our Commando trainer. He is a black belt in martial arts! You have to train with him if you want to come!' declares Harsh.

I take a good look at the black belt Love Commando. He

tries to look fierce, but he does not look particularly threatening, nor can he do much about his protruding stomach that spills several inches over his tight pants. I ask Harsh where the runaway couples stay and he points to the roof. I notice a rickety iron staircase near the entrance—it looks like this is the only way up. I ask if there are any couples in residence. He points to a pair of young women cooking in a kitchen attached to the office. Two other couples sit huddled around a black-and-white TV. They are not allowed to leave the cramped space without the permission of Harsh and Sanjoy.

I take a look around at the dismal conditions and ask them how they make enough money to sustain the organization. Suddenly Sanjoy looks gloomy and begins telling me his woes. They shot to fame after being featured in the media. Now they have hundreds of couples calling from across the country. They don't have the heart to deny them assistance, but they do not have the resources to house them either. They have had to sell their cars and houses to make ends meet. Sanjoy says that he has one piece of land left in his village which he will have to sell next if things don't work out. They receive some donations, but not enough. Sometimes lovers whom they have 'settled' send funds, but this is usually not the case. The ones who do give money are the journalists who come to interview them. Sanjoy takes out a carefully folded cheque from his pocket, and proudly shows it to me. He says that the $100 check is courtesy a Belgian journalist who has made a documentary on them. Harsh tells me with an eager smile that they are expecting something from me too.

As we are talking, a small man comes into the room with a box of white, milky sweets that he offers to us. Sanjoy tells me that this man had an inter-caste marriage against the wishes of his wife's parents, who kidnapped her after the marriage. The Love Commandos helped him get his wife back, so he has come to thank them.

Harsh has six cell phones, six different helpline numbers for lovers to call on. The phones ring continuously. Harsh picks up one phone and turns on the speaker for me to listen in.

The caller has a girlish, nasal voice. She is a student from Pune, called Pallavi.

'I am in love with the boy, what do I do?' she says squeakily.

Harsh: What is your age?

Pallavi: Nineteen.

Harsh: The boy's age?

Pallavi: Twenty-one.

Harsh: What does he do?

Pallavi: He works at a call centre.

Harsh: You want to get married?

Pallavi: Yes.

Harsh: Can you come to Delhi?

Pallavi: Uh...

Harsh: If you can come, tell me, if you can't come, tell me.

Pallavi: I want my parents to understand first.

Harsh: You want your parents to understand and then you want to get married? Or you want to get married anyways?

Pallavi: Uh...I don't know.

Harsh: How old is your love?

Pallavi: Seven years.

Harsh: When you first started your love, did you ask your parents? NO! The Indian Constitution says after eighteen the guardianship of your parents ends. You can do as you please.

Pallavi: My parents tell me they will commit suicide.

Harsh: Till date no parent has died, if anyone has died, then the lover has or the love dies. You have to raise your confidence, get married and come here. We will protect you from the problems.

Pallavi: My parents are asking me to come home but I am scared. My best friend was killed last month because she loved someone from outside her caste.

Harsh: Be confident. If your parents don't murder you, then they will do emotional atyachaar. When you want to get married, then you call us.

Harsh shakes his head in disgust when he puts down the phone. 'See, they killed her friend, they will kill her too. It's pretty standard. She has loved, so kill, that's the way the story always goes.'

Harsh and Sanjoy cite the example of the Manoj-Babli honour killing case. In June 2007, the killing of newly-weds Manoj and Babli was ordered by a khap panchayat in Kaithal district, Haryana, because they got married despite being from the same gotra or clan. Honour killings go both ways—for marrying outside the caste, or for marrying too deep within. The landmark case that followed convicted Babli's parents for the honour killing—a first in Indian history.

As in Manoj and Babli's case, often the killers are the lovers' families, in collusion with the khap panchayats of their village. Khap panchayats are kangaroo courts run by elderly men in villages and towns across India. These councils once dominated political life in villages across north India by exerting social control through edicts that governed everything from marriage to property disputes. Though several villages have grown into towns because of rapid urbanization and despite the fact that the Supreme Court has condemned these councils as illegal bodies, khap panchayats continue to thrive—a far from vestigial organ of the country's rural heritage.

A smattering of statements by various chaudharys or heads of the khap panchayats highlight their antediluvian views. The chaudhary of the Baliyan khap, Mahendra Singh Tikai, has gone on record saying, 'Love marriages are dirty, I don't even want to repeat the word, and only whores can choose their partners.' He further said, 'Same-gotra marriages are incestuous, incest violates maryada (honour) and villagers would kill or be killed to protect their maryada.' He scoffs at the laws of the Indian state, calling them 'the root of all problems'. 'That's your Constitution, ours is different.'

Amongst many other retrograde suggestions, the khaps have advocated child marriage, saying that if it is instituted, the natural sexual desires arising when the child hits puberty will be avoided, while another has said that girls should be married at the age of sixteen as it will help young people satisfy their sexual needs and will also help reduce rape cases. Some have suggested banning phones and jeans for women as a way to avoid titillation and rape, while another khap leader stated that chowmein caused hormonal imbalance which led to men raping women.

To make matters even more difficult for lovers, the police are widely distrusted, especially in the cow belt of India, in states like Uttar Pradesh, Bihar, Haryana and Punjab. Despite orders directing the police 'to deal sternly with parents/relatives/other members of the society who threaten such couples', and to provide 'mediation/counselling cells' and 'to prevail upon resisting parents/relatives to reconcile with such couples', people at large suspect the police to be in cahoots with the khap panchayats. This is where organizations like the Love Commandos are able to help. 'The Government is a fraud. They promised a bill against honour killings that has still not been passed. They know they will lose votes if they pass this. The khap panchayats control many votes. They even said they would get us [Love Commandos] involved, but we haven't gotten even one call!' exclaims Sanjoy in a fit of anger.

According to a 2006 survey, 'law enforcers as well as people (both rural and urban) in the affected states agreed that khaps were raising the right issues (81 per cent of the 300 police personnel interviewed and 46 per cent of the 600 residents)'. Even though young India is daring to fall in love, there is resistance from an older social order and this is why the awful khap panchayats have not been eradicated despite their terrible, misogynistic views.

Sanjoy sighs, suddenly looking tired after his burst of anger. He looks down at his shoes and says, 'It's sad, parents get so happy seeing filmi love stories, but when it comes to their own daughter's love, it's a different story.'

ten

~

# THE LOVERS*

## AMITAVA KUMAR

In America, the land of the free and home of the brave, it was possible, figuratively speaking, to examine genitalia in public.** I discovered this when I turned on the radio one day and heard a woman's voice. A foreign accent, except the surprise was that she was talking about sex. She sounded like Henry Kissinger. Her name was Dr Ruth. Unlike Kissinger, she wanted us to make love, not war.

In India, the only public mentions of sex were the advertisements painted on the walls that ran beside the railway tracks. I read the ads when I travelled from Patna to Delhi for college, and was filled with anxiety about

*Extracted from *The Lovers*

**Bill Clinton on President Obama's re-election: 'He's luckier than a dog with two dicks.' Of course, Bill Clinton deserves a footnote in any book on love. My writing notebook also has this quote in it: 'I—but you know, love can mean different things, too, Mr. Bittman. I have—there are a lot of women with whom I have never had any inappropriate conduct, who were friends of mine, who will say from time to time, "I love you". And I know that they don't mean anything wrong by that.' —Bill Clinton, Testimony Before Grand Jury.

what awaited me when, at last, I would experience sex. On the brick walls near the tracks, large white letters in Hindi urging you to call a phone number if you suffered from premature ejaculation or erectile dysfunction or nightly emissions. A nation of silent sufferers! Men with worried brows holding their heads in their offices during the day, and, back at home, lying miserably awake beside quiet and disappointed wives in the dark.

But not in America where Dr Ruth was talking to you cheerfully on the air. I had no accurate idea of what *epiglottis* and *guttural* really meant, but those words vibrated in my mind when I listened to Dr Ruth. Her voice on the small, black radio-cum-cassette-player in the privacy of my room offering advice to the males among her audience. Even if they themselves had already climaxed, they could help their female partners achieve orgasm.

—You can just pleasure her.

I hadn't heard that word used as a verb before. I also spoke in an accented English; I wondered if Dr Ruth's usage was correct.

—And for women out there, a man wants an orgasm. Big deal! Give him an orgasm, it takes two minutes!

*Such relief.* For more than one reason.

There were details about her that I discovered later. Dr Ruth grew up in an orphanage. Her parents perished at Auschwitz. She was very short but had fought in a war. She was once a guerrilla in the Haganah and now, in this country, she was famous for talking about masturbation and penises and vaginas on the radio. An extraordinary and busy life. She was on her third marriage.

You will understand when I say that listening to Dr Ruth that night in my room on Morningside Drive I was back in Delhi where it was morning and we were enjoying three days of spring. The year I left, 1990. My friends were in my room in the college dorm. The daughter of the warden walked past the window on her way to work, her hair still hanging damp on her yellow dupatta. She was a post-doc in history and would become a lecturer soon. And then we were running to the end of the corridor to watch the warden's daughter open the little wooden gate on her way to the bus stop. Her prepossessing calm, her very indifference to the existence of gawking others, was an incitement to collective lust. She was soon gone and, still excited but also somewhat let down, the group returned to my small room with its dirty, whitewashed walls.

—There is nothing purer than the love for your landlord's daughter, said Bheem.

—No, said Santosh, after an appropriate pause. If you are looking for innocence, the purest gangajal, you have to be in love with your teacher's wife.

As if to sort out the matter, we looked at Noni, a Sikh from Patiala. He was the only one amongst us who wasn't a virgin.

Noni took off his turban and his long hair fell over his shoulders.

—You bastards should stop pretending. The only true love, true first love, is the love for your maidservant.

This was duly appreciated. But Noni was not done yet.

—She has to be older than you, though not by too much, and while it's not necessary for you to have fucked her, it is important that she take your hand in hers and put it on her breast.

There was the usual silence that greets the utterance of grand truth. Three bodies were sprawled next to each other on the bed, their heads pillowed against the wall behind them. Aureoles of dark, oily smudges indicated where other heads had pressed against that wall. Then, someone started laughing.

—You are a bunch of pussies, Noni said, to dismiss the laughing. When you went back home during the winter, did any one of you get laid?

He smiled and announced his own success with another question.

—Has anyone slept with a friend's mother?

—I have, Bheem said. He had light-coloured eyes. He was smiling a soft, secret smile.

—Whose mother? Noni asked.

—Yours.

Noni was my Dr Ruth before Dr Ruth.. My naiveté was the price of admission I paid for his tutorials. Noni had discovered that the medical definition of a kiss was 'the anatomical juxtaposition of two orbicularis oris muscles in a state of contraction'. This made the unfamiliar even more unfamiliar. He told me that the word 'fuck' was an acronym derived from 'for unlawful carnal knowledge'; this terminology was itself a rewriting, Noni said, of the medieval rule to which 'fuck' owed its origins, 'fornication under consent of the King.' Noni was completely wrong; at that time, however, I marvelled at his knowledge of sex.

Until I met Noni in Delhi, my familiarity with sex was limited to what I had learned from the censored movies screened on Saturdays in Patna. I'd be sitting with others in the dark, the air warm, the smell of sweat around me, and somewhere a cigarette being smoked. There were probably two hundred others in the theatre, almost all men and most of them older than me. In the local paper the theatre advertised itself as 'air-cooled' but what you breathed was the effluvia of restless groins shifting in fixed seats that had coir-stuffing poking out of torn rexine covers. It was no doubt cooler in the apartment in Prague where the on-screen action was taking place. A middle-aged man had unclasped the hook of the bra that an impossibly young woman was wearing. She turned to face him, her breasts milk-white, with pale pink drowsy nipples. There was a cut and a jump in the film there. The duo was now in an open car on an empty road, driving under leafy trees, in bright sunlight.

But a child had started crying in the audience near me.

—*Scene dikha, baccha ro raha hai*, a man shouted from a further seat, wanting us to return to the bedroom. 'Show a breast. Because if you don't [offer the nipple], the baby will cry.' The rough remark, bewildering at that time, soon lost its confusing aspect: glinting like mica in a piece of granite, it sat for a while in the nostalgic narrative about my late teenage years.

Ten years later, for the benefit of a later generation, a sex advice column in *Mumbai Mirror* had become popular in India. I made this discovery when my laundry came back to my hotel room wrapped in newspaper.

Q. *My girlfriend kissed the tip of my penis and the next day she suffered a stomach-ache. Could she be pregnant? Should she take some pills?*

A. She must have had dinner afterwards and that probably led to the stomach-ache. Oral sex does not cause pregnancy and she need not take any pills.

Q. *I am a 25-year-old man. Please tell me if regular masturbation can increase the size of one's butt.*

A. Just as your nose, fingers and tongue will not increase in size, neither will the butt.

Q. *When it comes to sex, my partner allows me to use only a finger for just a few seconds. Please tell me why. Also, when I hold my bowels for too long, my testicles swell and hurt. What could be the reason for this?*

The good doctor, the Sexpert, had once again exercised a grim matter-of-factness, the humour in his eyes hidden under the thick glasses he wore in the grainy photograph.

A. She is probably scared by your intentions—pregnancy or an infection. Why not ask her? And, do you mean 'balls'? 'Bowels' refers to the intestines. Why would you want to hold them? Please explain.

The *New York Times* carried a story on the Sexpert. His name is Dr Mahinder Watsa and he recently turned ninety-three. His editor says the doctor has received more than 40,000 letters seeking advice. He has tried to promote sex education but many of his own colleagues say it is pornography. Dr Watsa was the first to use words like penis and vagina in the newspapers. A reader filed an obscenity suit against the doctor, charging that the editors fabricated letters to increase readership. In response, the editor delivered a sack of unopened letters at the judge's table. 'He read them over the lunch hour and dismissed the case.'

The Sexpert column can now be read on the Internet. There was nothing like this when I was growing up in India. If, at the time, I could have written one, which letter would have been mine? The range of problems people present to the doctor is stunning but yes, this one:

*Q. In the last semester, I failed one subject. My parents got worried and took me to an astrologer. He asked me to remove my pants. He said the ejaculate after masturbation is equal to 100 ml of blood, hence my weakness. I am regretting showing him my penis. Please help.*

A. The astrologer is a hoax and completely ignorant of sexual matters. Masturbation is completely normal. Visit your college counsellor instead to discuss your not doing well in one subject.

eleven

~

# THE BOOK OF CHOCOLATE SAINTS*

## JEET THAYIL

---

The taxi took them to the house of a journalist Goody knew from her time in the city. Paro took immediate charge. They were to rest from their travels and familiarize themselves with the city while she found them an apartment to rent. For now they had a guest room facing a stand of frangipani trees and Paro threw a small party that she called a get-together.

It was the time of tsunamis and bombs.

The day before three explosions had occurred in the city's most populous shopping district and in the news photos Goody noted, as always, the women's shoes and slippers strewn over the bombsite.

'So there are monuments in Delhi, so what?' a transplanted Bombayite told Goody.

The woman had moved to Delhi when she married.

*Extracted from *The Book of Chocolate Saints*

She'd been a professional party-thrower in Bombay, a job she called event management. She was still throwing parties but for a classier crowd.

'If every second fool made a monument to himself in Bombay we'd also have thousands of them. I moved here because, what, capital city, has to be more secure, right? Wrong! You're out buying jeans, which, just remember, you're buying cheap jeans, and dishoom you wake up legless in a hospital.'

'How long have you been here?'

'Let's see, eight, no, nine years. My god, has it already been that long? I think I need another gin-tonic.'

'Nine years and you still sound like a Bombayite.'

'Darling, I hope I never sound like a Dilliwalli.'

Goody heard this a lot, how awful the city was, how inhospitable, how unsafe for women. But Delhi was her town. It was where she had grown up and where she returned after she left London and she wanted to show it off to Xavier.

People filled their plates with samosas, kebabs, and paneer on skewers. They sipped punch from shot glasses and gossiped about the Gandhis.

It was the time of tsunamis and bombs.

'Paharganj, Govindpuri, Sarojini Nagar,' said Sonia Grover, a lawyer who knew more secrets about politicians and industrialists than most journalists. She was a friend of Goody's mother. 'See what places they target. Markets where the middle class and the working class do their Diwali shopping. Why not pick on the rich?'

'I'm sure they will,' said Goody.

'Not that I'm complaining but pick on someone your own size, you get me?'

'I get you, but it's penis size that's the real problem. The bombs, the rage, the religious screeching, all that is compensation.'

'You're a woman now. I remember you as a schoolgirl. How temperamental you were, endearingly anti-social. Your mother didn't know what to do with you.'

'That may be the perfect epitaph for me. Her mother didn't know what to do with her and neither did she. And you know what, I think I might be a little anti-social still.'

'You artistic types,' said Sonia. 'What can I say?'

She patted her hair and downed a shot of punch. Immediately Paro brought around a tray of glasses filled to the brim and Sonia took another. She shook Goody's hand in a businesslike way and went to a group of men smoking on the balcony.

Goody found Xavier in the bedroom, alone, staring at the only decoration on the walls, a poster of Gauguin's Jacob wrestling with a yellow-winged angel on a flat ground of vivid red. It wasn't the wrestlers he was looking at, but the peasant women in the foreground. He seemed entranced.

'No,' he said, his eyes on the poster. 'I think, I don't think I can go out there. I have nothing to say. I'm dry as a bone. I want a shared spiritual experience not a wrestling match.'

She made excuses to the guests. He was train-weary and crotchety, she said. Coming down with something, Delhi belly, maybe, or chikungunya or dengue. Who knows? He'll be out at some point, I'm sure. Best to just let him be.

But he did not come out. He stayed in the room until long after the last of them had left. He was doing nothing, as far as she could see, other than staring at the Gauguin, the peasant women in their white bonnets sharing some kind of religious experience, their eyes shut and hands folded in prayer, their great pale heads lovingly detailed in comparison to the indistinct figures of Jacob and the angel.

Their arrival in the city coincided with a downturn or upturn in Xavier's condition. With the medication taking hold he was no longer excitable. Sometimes she missed his manic phase. Was it better for him to be energized and falling for a procession of young women, or depressed and not producing? Undoubtedly the former but it made him unmanageable.

To get him out of the house she rented a car and they went

to the Q'utb Minar. They kept the driver waiting and walked towards the structure, which was roofed and pillared but open on all sides. At the centre was a narrow tomb of faded marble. The Q'utb's lack of doors and oversight had extracted a price. Names had been scratched into the tomb. There was graffiti on the walls and grillwork. There were lists of all kinds.

*Ronita I love you.*

*Kuldeep I love you.*

*Neha loves herself.*

*I love you Kavita but you don't love me Bhola.*

*Deepak, Neetu, Dhiraj I love you.*

*Dial 36219837 and enjoy.*

And at the end of these oddly promissory slogans was one in the past tense. *Mansoor loved Afsana.*

'Love,' Goody said.

'This was once the tallest tower in ancient India,' said Xavier, who had perked up in the presence of ancient buildings. 'The strict lines and clean shape? It's the Muslim architectural line, human separated from divine and only the divine worthy of consecration.'

'Do you think we'll learn to love each other again?'

Without waiting for a reply, she walked ahead to a television monitor. For twenty rupees it gave you the view from a video camera attached to the top of the Q'utb. They were close enough to the tower to see the fine work on its upper storeys, the marble and red sandstone, but the monitor showed live action footage of the unexceptional buildings nearby. Goody saw a sign, Remote Presence Facilitation System. Such a grand name for a camera pointed the wrong way. When they reached the Quwwatul adjacent to the Q'utb she felt a little faint, like a woman in a nineteenth-century novel. The words 'smelling salts' came into her head, though it was water she wanted. The question she had asked came back to her like a cave echo.

'The oldest extant mosque in India,' Xavier said in his

special voice, 'and one of the oldest indications of Hindu–Muslim collaboration and competition, which is what makes for the charged architecture.'

He seemed to have revived, or he was making an effort. He had revived and she had wilted. They edged around massive stone screens inscribed with geometric designs. She caught sight of the inner masjid, the perimeter supported by dozens of stone pillars, like no Muslim building she had seen. There was a proliferation of deities and the abundant female figures found on temple walls.

'But it looks so Hindu,' she said.

A plaque said the mosque's cloisters had been built using pillars, carved columns 'and other architectural members' of twenty-seven Hindu and Jain temples taken in their entirety to the site of the Q'utb.

'In other words, the temples were destroyed to make this. Do you see?' Xavier said, running a hand along a pillar. 'More to it than the linear Islamic ache that sublimates desire into calligraphy.'

'That's what I like about you, New, you're better than a guidebook. Right now? I think I like you more than I have for a long time.'

'Touch it and feel how the pillar curves. Now look up there, see those supports? What's surprising about them? You're not looking. Yes, exactly, four men, facing in four directions. The human figure in a mosque, how did they get away with it?'

The figures were male, Aryan, kingly. They lay against the ceiling, knees bent and dangling upward, looking down at the viewer, the entire figure a refutation of gravity. Each had been given some individualized characterization, the Brahmin thread or armlets or royal headgear, and there wasn't a flat belly among them. Goody thought: Indian stomachs.

'Take a look at the faces. See how they've been hacked with such force that some part of the chest is missing as well?'

'Look,' she said, excited. 'There are female figures too.'

'But fewer, as if they were slipped in when no one was looking.'

The women too had come under the hacker's sword and not a face or breast had been left unharmed. But the destroyers had been in a hurry; some loveliness was still visible in the parts that remained.

Later they drove through the streets of the old city to the Lal Qila. Goody asked the driver to put the windows up. She felt the pollution in her chest and throat. She would carry a handkerchief to spit in, she thought, like a consumptive. She would be one of those women who walked around with a perfumed hankie pressed to the nose, asking for smelling salts. The taxi had to make a U-turn and then it stopped in a crush of autorickshaws, trucks, and Blue Line buses. Ahead of them was a black Ambassador with a sign painted on its back in rural red and yellow. HORAN PLEEJ. They were trapped in a corridor of cars and buses and the driver pressed pointlessly on the horn.

A woman came to the window with her pallu over her head. She had big lips, like Goody's, and her lipstick was a similar shade of brown. She stared and Goody stared back. In one expert glance the woman took in their clothes, the car, their potential generosity. There was a blond boy of two or three on her hip, a thin child playing with a rubber band. Her blouse was wet from two spreading stains where she'd suckled him and Goody had a sudden desire to taste the woman's breast milk. The extended family was camped on the pavement. The men lounged at their ease and smoked, healthier and cleaner than their wives who sold trinkets and begged and raised the children. A girl of three or four left the group and went to a Maruti with a couple in the front. The woman with the blond baby shook her head and the girl moved to a bigger car. The woman came to Xavier's window but she didn't ask for money. She held her baby to him as if in offering and Xavier gave her a note. Her smile was sweet and shy.

Then the traffic cleared and they neared the walls of the

great fort, its ramparts converted into a traffic underpass. At the entrance they squeezed past a crush of loiterers and guides and in a corridor of shops she found a framed painting of Ganesh in the pose of a Mughal emperor. He had his arm around a seated woman whose veil had come undone and his trunk was in a state of semi-arousal. Goody considered buying it but the thought of haggling with the salesman was beyond her. She wanted a fixed price. She wanted a cold drink and air-conditioning. She wanted silence and a nap in a dark room.

They went to the pavilion where the emperor met with his public. A guard with a rifle and fixed bayonet stood in front of the only object in the fort that was still intact, the throne with its inlay of birds and green leaves. Some inlay remained at the Khas Mahal but most of the silver and gold had been vandalized. Near the octagonal tower where the emperor made an appearance every morning there was a latticework door that had rotted at the hinges. Goody noticed that its great feature had survived, two tiny brass elephants whose heads served as handles, the elephants and their mahouts superbly energized and bursting with detail. The trunks formed a loop into which she placed her index finger and she traced the head with her thumb and felt something of the power the artist must have felt as he worked.

The centrepiece of the building was a screen with the image of a pair of scales. Not a panel remained, only a set of discolourations on the wall. The mirror and marble inlay, the gold and silver ceiling work—all had been stolen. Goody asked a soldier if they could take a look at a roped-off section. Area is closed, he said. Then, addressing her breasts, he pointed out which parts of the palace were open for viewing. When she backed away he scratched his genitals with great care, as if the gesture would seduce her on the spot.

twelve

~

# DILDAR BEGUM AND A MARRIAGE PROPOSAL*

## IRA MUKHOTY

---

When Humayun reaches the ancient town of Paat, Hindal's mother Dildar Begum arranges for a 'grand entertainment' in which all the members of this fractured court are able to come and greet their dispossessed padshah. Included in this party is a fourteen-year-old girl, native to the town of Paat, Hamida Banu Begum. She is the daughter of Hindal's preceptor, Shaikh Ali Akbar Jami, who is himself a descendant of a Shi'a sage known by the awe-inspiring sobriquet of His Reverence the Terrible Elephant. 'Who is this?' asks Humayun when he sees the young girl, clearly smitten by her beauty and grace. Hamida Banu is often to be found visiting Hindal's haraman in Dildar Begum's company, and it is not long before Humayun indicates to his stepmother his desire to marry the young Hamida Banu. But the thirty-two year-old, battle-scarred and already much married

*Extracted from *Daughters of the Sun*

Mughal pretender is probably an underwhelming proposition for the very young Hamida Banu and she initially refuses to consider Humayun's proposal. Even Hindal is angry at Humayun's behaviour, quite probably believing that with Sher Shah Suri and Shah Husain Mirza as immediate dangers, it was hardly the time for Humayun to be considering matrimony. 'I look on this girl as a sister and child of my own,' says Hindal angrily to Humayun, now reminding him of his impoverished condition and the need to produce a suitable mahr or bride gift. 'You are a king. Heaven forbid there should not be a proper alimony.' But Humayun is annoyed at these objections and asks Dildar Begum to intercede on his behalf. 'As for what they have written about alimony,' he pleads with her, desperately and somewhat unrealistically, given his circumstances, 'please Heaven, what they ask will be done.' Dildar Begum acknowledges the patience and tact required in such a situation and advises Humayun to stay calm. 'It is astonishing that you should go away in anger over a few words', she tells him. Dildar must also handle her son Hindal's objections and, according to Jauhar, she rebukes Hindal: 'You are speaking very improperly to his Majesty, whom you ought to consider the representative of your late father.'

To Hamida Banu herself, Dildar is gentle and pragmatic. 'After all you will marry someone,' Dildar tells the young girl. 'Better than a king, who is there?' And this is the prosaic reality of a girl's choices which Dildar wants Hamida Banu to understand. It is an eloquent testimony of Hamida Banu's wit and spirit that she is said to have replied: 'Oh yes, I shall marry someone,' she admits to Dildar, with bracing candour, 'but he shall be a man whose collar my hand can touch and not one whose skirt it does not reach.' If Humayun is a king, Hamida Banu argues, then he is too exalted a person for her and she would rather marry someone closer to her own standing in society. Humayun persists, and asks Dildar to send Hamida Banu to see him. But the young girl refuses, questioning Humayun's motive and invoking propriety:

'If it is to pay my respects, I was exalted by paying my respects the other day,' she tells Humayun tartly, before adding, 'why should I come again?' But after forty days, with the sympathetic Dildar's efforts, Hamida Banu finally agrees to the proposal and she is married to Humayun. A mahr of two lakhs is given to the bride. Hamida Banu could never have imagined, as a young fourteen-year-old, how irrevocable her decision would be and how precipitous the changes that it would bring to her life.

The many intimate details we know of Hamida Banu's brusque courtship by Humayun is because the two young sisters-in-law, Gulbadan and Hamida Banu, will become very close friends later in life. When Gulbadan writes her biography more than forty years later, many of the incidents will have been told to her by Hamida Banu herself, still sharp in the women's minds almost half a century later and long after Humayun himself is dead. It is in the audacious memory of Gulbadan's biography that we have an intermittent view into the many human emotions and the domestic politics that lay behind the grander scope of the Mughals' canvas. The small fallibilities and unexpected weaknesses and through it all the complex network of female influence that allowed life to carry on in the most desperate and unusual of circumstances. This particular incident, with its irresolute bride and harried groom will, of course, have particularly far-reaching consequences as it will result in the birth of Akbar, the greatest of the great Mughals.

The immediate future for Humayun and Hamida Banu, however, is decidedly more prosaic and holds only uncertainty and betrayals. The newly-wed couple travels to Bhakkar along with Humayun's much depleted and battered army, hoping to gain a foothold in the district of Sehwana. Shah Husain Mirza continues to pursue Humayun through Sind with deadly intent, and all the while Humayun's few remaining officers surreptitiously desert the increasingly frayed Mughal camp whenever they can. So piteous is Humayun's situation that at one point he stays up all night to physically prevent any potential deserters from leaving him. In the morning, his great amirs Tardi Beg and Munim Beg, somewhat farcically, try and run towards their horses to make a getaway while Humayun is bathing, and the Padshah Ghazi of Hindustan has to run after them himself, admonishing and pleading, till they have no choice but to remain with their padshah, albeit with bad grace.

For Humayun and Hamida Banu, meanwhile, the erratic and hopeless wandering continues. They lack basic supplies, sometimes foraging for wild berries or seizing supplies of grain and provisions from errant caravans like common thieves. Finally, and by this time Hamida Banu is seven months pregnant, Raja Maldeo of Jodhpur invites them to Rajasthan where they are relieved to find at least some grain and water. But the onward march through the desert of Rajasthan is gruelling and it is a 'horrid journey' in which 'many of our people died, and all suffered exceedingly', writes Jauhar grimly. Upon reaching the territory of Maldeo, moreover, Humayun finds that there is 'no act of hospitality being shown us or any comfort given to the distressed monarch'. The raja, 'that ravening demon' as the ever bombastic Abu'l-Fazl has it, instead makes 'idle excuses' and sends a rather derisory present of fruit. All this while, Humayun's retainers continue to desert him and the mood in the Mughal camp is one of anxiety and bleak despondency. 'If you leave me, whither will you go?' the unhappy Humayun asks his retainers. 'You have no other refuge.' But while Humayun's followers continue to leave him for better prospects, the ones who truly have no other refuge, and must follow him through this landscape of the damned, are his haraman, and the diminished party now disconsolately marches on into the desert. Hamida Banu, now a heavily pregnant fifteen-year-old, rides on horseback in the unforgiving desert heat while the other women manage as best they can, on foot or on camel. 'Many women and men were on foot,' admits Jauhar. They head towards Umerkot, in heat so fierce the 'horses and other quadrupeds kept sinking to the knees in the sand'.

The Mughal party proceeds westwards, harried not only by the heat, the thirst and the hunger, but also by querulous chieftains and Rajput rajas who sense the increasing vulnerability of Humayun and attack him whenever they get a chance. Humayun sends his great amirs onwards, to divert the attention of the marauders, and himself remains with his female companions and servants. His amirs are attacked and resolve to 'sell our lives as dearly as possible' but in the end, Humayun's officer, Shaikh Ali Beg, is able to hustle the attacking soldiers and decapitates two of their chiefs, bringing the heads as macabre trophies to bolster Humayun's faltering resolve. The few wells Humayun's party are able to find are filled up with sand, apparently on Raja Maldeo's orders, so that when water is found at last, the soldiers and servants and animals are desperate with thirst. 'The misery we suffered at this stage,' admits Jauhar, 'was intolerable.'

When water is found at last in these wells, buckets are lowered and 'people flung themselves on it; the ropes broke, and five or six persons fell into the wells with the buckets. Many perished from thirst.' Humayun passes around his own water bottle to try and control his retainers and appeals to his amir Tardi Beg 'in the Turky language', with considerable grace, given the circumstances, to 'be so good as draw off your people for a short time from the well till mine are served, which will prevent disputes'. By this stage, there are hardly any horses left with the Mughal party, only a few sturdy mules and camels. Not far from Umerkot, finding himself short of a horse, one of Humayun's officers unchivalrously demands his horse back from Hamida Banu. Humayun, now only accompanied by seven horsemen, then gives his own horse to his wife and mounts a camel belonging to a water carrier.

In these miserly circumstances, the bedraggled party arrive at Umerkot to be given a civil reception by Raja Rana Prasad. 'The day was not a fortunate one,' says the raja with courteous understatement, hoping that 'on the following day he would mount the throne.' The raja assigns Humayun 'excellent quarters' inside the fort while the amirs pitch their tents in the pleasant surroundings of the fort amidst greenery and water tanks. So reduced is Humayun's situation that he only has the clothes on his back. When he gives his clothes to be washed, he must wait in his dressing gown till they are ready to be worn. Hamida Banu's situation, now in the final months of her pregnancy, can hardly have been much better. While Humayun is waiting in his tent in his dressing gown, a beautiful bird becomes trapped inside the tent. Humayun captures the bird, snips off a feather before releasing it, and then has the feather painted by an artist in his entourage. It is hardly an unremarkable fact that even in his depleted, meagre following, Humayun has a painter accompanying him. There is a glitter, already, of the later magnificence of the Mughal's miniature painters. Hamida Banu, meanwhile, finds that provisions can at last be bought, however, and goats are found to be very cheap, only one rupee for four goats. 'Several days,' says Gulbadan, clearly echoing Hamida Banu's satisfaction, 'were spent in peace and comfort.' For a few weeks, at least, Hamida Banu is able to rest in relative comfort and security for these last months of her pregnancy.

After seven weeks, Humayun prepares to leave for Jun, near the Rann of Kutch. Hamida Banu remains at Umerkot with the rest of Humayun's haraman, under the care of her brother Khwaja Muazzam. Three days later, on 15 October 1542, a son is born to Hamida Banu. When the news is conveyed to Humayun, he is overjoyed and breaks a pod of musk which he distributes amongst his chiefs and amirs saying, 'This is all the present I can afford to make you on the birth of my son, whose fame will I trust be one day expanded all over the world, as the perfume of the musk now fills this apartment.' This son he now gives the name he had once heard in his dream—Jalaluddin Muhammad Akbar.

# ACKNOWLEDGEMENTS

Grateful acknowledgement is made to these copyright holders for permission to reprint copyrighted material in this volume:

'Object' is extracted from *I Speak for the Devil* by Imtiaz Dharker (Bloodaxe, 2001), reprinted by permission of the publisher (www.bloodaxebooks.com); 'A Suitable Boy' is extracted from *A Suitable Boy* by Vikram Seth (1993), reprinted by permission of the author; 'Tang' by Saadat Hasan Manto translated by Nasreen Rehman (2019), reprinted by permission of the translator; 'A Little Kitten' by Kamala Das (1992), reprinted by permission of the Estate of Kamala Das; 'Laajwanti' by Rajinder Singh Bedi is extracted from *An Epic Unwritten* translated by Muhammad Umar Memon (Penguin Books India, 1998), reprinted by permission of the publisher; 'Taj' is extracted from *Taj* by Timari N. Murari (1985), reprinted by permission of the author; 'Desolation, Lust' by Upamanyu Chatterjee (1986), reprinted by permission of the author; *The Deepest Blue* by K. R. Meera translated by J. Devika (2005), reprinted by permission of the author and translator; 'Stolen' is extracted from *A Pleasant Kind of Heavy and Other Erotic Stories* by Amrita Narayanan (Aleph, 2013), reprinted by permission of the author; 'Love Revolution' is extracted from *India in Love* by Ira Trivedi (Aleph, 2014), reprinted by permission of the author; 'The Lovers' is extracted from *The Lovers* by Amitava Kumar (Aleph, 2017), reprinted by permission of the author; 'The Book of Chocolate Saints' is extracted from *The Book of Chocolate Saints* by Jeet Thayil (Aleph, 2017), reprinted by permission of the author; and 'Dildar Begum and a Marriage Proposal' is extracted from *Daughters of the Sun* by Ira Mukhoty (Aleph, 2018), reprinted by permission of the author.

# NOTES ON THE CONTRIBUTORS

**Rajinder Singh Bedi** (1915–1984) wrote many successful plays and established himself as a highly nuanced fiction writer with the publication of *Daana-o-Daam*, his first collection of short stories. He produced and wrote scripts for a number of successful films. His Urdu novel, *Ek Chaadar Maili Si*, translated into English by Khushwant Singh as *I Take This Woman*, received the Sahitya Akademi Award in 1965.

**Upamanyu Chatterjee** (born 1959) joined the Indian Administrative Service in 1983. His published works include short stories and the novels *English, August: An Indian Story*, *The Last Burden*, *The Mammaries of the Welfare State*, which won the Sahitya Akademi Award for Writing in English, *Weight Loss*, *Way to Go* and *Fairy Tales at Fifty* and the recent novella, *The Revenge of the Non-Vegetarian*. In 2008, he was awarded the Officier of Ordre des Arts et des Lettres by the French Government for his contribution to literature.

**Kamala Das** (1934–2009) also wrote as Madhavikutty, and later changed her name to Surayya. She wrote novels, poetry and short stories in English and Malayalam. She received the Kerala Sahitya Akademi Award, Sahitya Akademi Award, Valayar Award and Kent Award for English Writing from Asian Countries. She was nominated in 1984 for the Nobel Prize in Literature.

**J. Devika** (born 1968) is a a writer, translator, feminist, teacher and researcher at the Centre for Development Studies, Kerala. Her main areas of interest are the history of gender, development, and culture and politics of Kerala. She employs an interdisciplinary approach in her research, and many of her articles have been published in international, national and regional journals. Her most notable translations include short stories by Sarah Joseph and K. R. Meera, and the autobiography of Nalini Jameela. She translated K. R. Meera's *Aarachaar* (*Hangwoman*) which won widespread acclaim.

**Amitava Kumar** (born 1963) is the author of *The Lovers*; *A Matter of Rats: A Short Biography of Patna*; *Home Products*, which was shortlisted for the Crossword Prize; and *A Foreigner Carrying in the Crook of His Arm a Tiny Bomb*, which received the Page Turner Award. Kumar's writing has appeared in *The Caravan*, *Harper's*, *The Guardian*, *New Yorker*, *Vanity Fair* and the *New York Times*. His essay 'Pyre', first published in *Granta*, was selected by Jonathan Franzen for *Best American Essays 2016*. He was awarded a Guggenheim Fellowship in 2016. Kumar is a Professor of English at Vassar College.

**Saadat Hasan Manto** (1912–1955) is regarded as the subcontinent's pre-eminent modern Urdu short fiction writer. He was a brilliant and prolific innovator. Of all Urdu fiction writers, he was the one who contributed the largest number of consistently high quality and equally controversial creative work to the Partition corpus. Manto was posthumously awarded the Nishaan-e-Imtiaaz by the Government of Pakistan.

**K. R. Meera** (born 1970) is an award-winning Malayalam writer. She worked as a journalist for the *Malayala Manorama*, but resigned to focus on her writing. Her first short story collection, *Ormayude Njarambu,* was followed by more short story collections, novellas, novels and children's books. She is the recipient of multiple awards, including the Sahitya Akademi Award in 2015 for her most famous novel *Aarachaar* (*Hangwoman*). It was shortlisted for the 2016 DSC Prize for South Asian Literature and won the Kerala Sahitya Akademi Award in 2013, as well as other regional awards.

**Muhammad Umar Memon** (1939–2018) was a critic, short story writer and translator of numerous works of Urdu fiction, most recently of the bestselling *The Greatest Urdu Stories Ever Told*. He was editor of the *Annual of Urdu Studies* (1993–2014).

**Ira Mukhoty** (born 1969) is the bestselling author of *Daughters of the Sun: Empresses, Queens and Begums of the Mughal Empire* and *Heroines: Powerful Indian Women of Myth and History*. She was educated in Delhi and Cambridge.

**Timeri N. Murari** (born 1941) is an award-winning writer, filmmaker and playwright. *Time* magazine chose his film *Daayraa* as one of its top ten films of 1996. His novel *Taj: A Story of Mughal India* has been translated into twenty-five languages.

**Amrita Narayanan** is a clinical psychologist and Homi Bhabha Fellow based in Goa. She is the editor of *The Parrots of Desire: 3,000 Years of Indian Erotica* and author of *A Pleasant Kind of Heavy and Other Erotic Stories* (a finalist for the Shakti Bhatt First Book Award) and of numerous essays on psychoanalysis, women and sexuality that have been published in India, the UK and US.

**Nasreen Rehman** is an award-winning screenwriter who has worked with directors such as Yash Chopra, Deepa Mehta and Mehreen Jabbar. *Kaifi and I* (2010), her translation of Shaukat Kaifi's memoir, was a bestseller.

**Vikram Seth** (born 1952) is the acclaimed author of three novels: *The Golden Gate*, *An Equal Music* and *A Suitable Boy*, one of the most beloved and widely read books of recent times. He has also published several books of poetry, an opera libretto, a book of other libretti, and two highly regarded works of non-fiction, *From Heaven Lake* and *Two Lives*. He is presently at work on *A Suitable Girl*.

**Jeet Thayil** (born 1959) worked as a journalist for twenty-three years before writing his first novel. His five poetry collections include *Collected Poems*, *English*, and *These Errors Are Correct*, which won the 2013 Sahitya Akademi Award. He is the editor of *The Bloodaxe Book of Contemporary Indian Poets*. Jeet Thayil's novel *Narcopolis* won the 2012 DSC Prize for South Asian Literature, and was shortlisted for five other prizes, including the Man Booker Prize, the Man Asian Literature Prize and the Commonwealth Prize. His latest novel is *The Book of Chocolate Saints*.

**Ira Trivedi** is the bestselling author of *India in Love: Marriage and Sexuality in the 21st Century*, *Nikhil and Riya*, *Gumrah: 11 Short Teen Crime Stories*, *There's No Love on Wall Street*, *The Great Indian Love Story* and *What Would You Do to Save the World?*. She has a BA from Wellesley College, an MBA from Columbia University and an LLB.